My interest in the Great [War began] many years apart. The first [was] when I was still a boy; he [gave me] John Ellis' excellent account of life on the Western Front, *Eye-deep in Hell*. The second was the discovery years later, by my father, of letters, photographs and a diary belonging to his grandfather; a man who, it transpired, had served in the 1/18th London Regiment (London Irish Rifles) during the Great War.

I was both fascinated and moved when I read those letters, and I determined to discover more about the war, his part in it, and the social context within which it was fought. I spent several years indulging my passion for the Great War: visiting the battlefields; attending talks and events; enjoying the opportunity of discussing the War with knowledgeable enthusiasts.

Having gathered a wealth of information on the War, I wondered how best to use it. There are plenty of non-fiction books about the Great War gracing the shelves of most bookshops; I have many of them. But I wanted to make the history of the War more accessible.

My stories, then, are historically accurate, although fictional, accounts; the stories of the men, and boys, who fought alongside my great-grandfather and brought about a momentous victory through determination, courage, and, perhaps, humour in adversity.

A J Warren

OVER BY CHRISTMAS
THE RETREAT FROM MONS

Happy 51st, Ian

30.11.15

Andy

A J WARREN

The Scribbler (DOTBIZ) Limited

For George

Preface

The Great War was a conflict that was fought between the major world powers at the beginning of the twentieth century. It began in the summer of 1914. Few people expected the conflict to last beyond Christmas; they were wrong. The war continued for over four years until November 1918, when the combatants agreed a truce known as the Armistice. By the end of the war, over sixteen million people had died, four empires had fallen and the face of the world had changed forever.

The war was fought between two groups of countries: the British (including the countries of her empire: Australia, Canada, India, New Zealand, Newfoundland), French, Belgian, Italian, Russian, Romanian, Serbian and later, the United States forces were known as the Allies. The German, Austro-Hungarian, Bulgarian and Ottoman (modern Turkey and her empire) forces formed the Central Powers.

When most people think of the Great War, they think probably of trenches, rats and mud; of a static war of attrition between two great armies with generals throwing their men forwards at a walking pace against barbed wire, artillery shells and machine-gun fire. By Christmas 1914, that's pretty much how it was. But it didn't start that way.

The Germans had a plan with which they intended to defeat France quickly, leaving her main allies, Britain and Russia, to fight on, fatally weakened without France, or to give in to Germany. This plan called for the Germans to sweep through Belgium and hook around the top of Paris, encircling the French armies. So, in the summer of 1914, enormous armies, millions of men strong, mobilized and swept across Europe.

The opening skirmishes and battles were nothing like those of the later years of the war; they bore a closer resemblance to the battles of the 19th Century that occurred in almost the same place a century before when Napoleon met Wellington at Waterloo. This novel tells the story of those opening clashes.

*

When the British Expeditionary Force (BEF) left for France in August 1914, it consisted of six infantry divisions and one cavalry division; around one hundred thousand men. Compared with the enormous standing armies of Europe, the BEF was tiny. But what it lacked in numbers, it made up for in training and professionalism.

Because our story concerns the cavalry, it is worth considering the structure of the Cavalry Division that went to war in that long, hot summer. The smallest unit of men was called a section and consisted of eight men commanded by a non-commissioned officer (NCO), usually a corporal. Four sections combined to create a troop, commanded by a subaltern (a 2nd lieutenant or lieutenant) and helped by a troop sergeant. Four troops made a squadron, commanded by a major (with a captain as second in command), and three squadrons made up a regiment of cavalry, commanded by a lieutenant-colonel. Each regiment had its own machine-gun section with two Vickers guns, and when at full complement, a cavalry regiment was about four hundred men strong.

A brigadier-general commanded a cavalry brigade; this unit was comprised three cavalry regiments, engineers, field ambulances, a veterinary section and one battery of horse artillery. The horse artillery battery of three sections consisted five officers, 200 men, 228 horses and six guns. A gun, its horses and men are called a sub-section and two sub-sections combine to create a section.

Four such brigades were grouped as a cavalry division. The Cavalry Division in August 1914 was commanded by Major-General Edmund Allenby.

In dreary, doubtful, waiting hours,
Before the brazen frenzy starts,
The horses show him nobler powers;
O patient eyes, courageous hearts!

Seventh verse of 'Into Battle'
by Julian Grenfell, DSO, Royal Dragoons.
Died of wounds, 26th May 1915

One

'Seven.' Richard tapped his piece on the board as he counted aloud. 'Bugger.'

'Richard!'

'Sorry, Mum.'

Harry laughed. 'That's the third time you've landed on that snake, Richard.'

Richard sighed, and slid his piece down the offending reptile.

'Have you fired a gun yet, Richard?' said Harry.

'Many times. We spend our time riding out onto the range for practise. It's a rare sight, too. The horses galloping over the downs, the men alongside, bringing the guns into action as fast as we can. And then we limber up and gallop away.'

'I'd love to join up.'

His mother shook her head. 'No, Harry. You're doing so well at school. You've got to take those exams. You can do so much with your life if you just can get a decent education, and Wilson's is a very good school.' She turned to Richard. 'Mr MacDowell says Harry stands a good chance of going to university.'

'Clever lad. Mum's right – you must keep at your studies, Harry.'

'Dad wants me to get a job. You know he does, Mum.'

Richard frowned. 'Bugger him. It's your life, Harry, and you mustn't let him tell you what to do.'

'That's easy for you to say. You got out. He's no control over you. I'm living in his house. How am I supposed to …'

'Now, don't worry about it, Harry. I'll deal with your father. And Richard? I'll thank you to keep your barrack room language out of this house.'

'Sorry.'

'My go,' said their mother, scooping up the dice and popping them into the shaker. She turned at the sound of the kitchen door closing. 'That's your father,' she said, reaching for the pieces on the board.

'Hang on, Mum, we haven't finished,' said Richard, putting out a hand to stop her.

'We'll play again tomorrow when your father's at work.'

'No. We won't; we're playing now.'

The sitting room door flew open and crashed into the end of the sofa.

'Ah,' said their father, 'the warrior returns.' He stared at the three of them sitting cross-legged around the Snakes and Ladders board on the floor before the fire. 'Tiddlywinks too much of a challenge for you, boy?'

Richard stood. 'Hello, Father.'

Their father frowned at the roaring blaze in the grate. 'I hope someone's going to pay for the coal. We're not made of money, you know, what with you off playing soldiers and Harry busy learning Latin.'

'It was cold, Dad,' said Harry.

'Shut up. If I want your opinion, I'll ask for it, boy.'

'How about a beer, dear?' said their mother, getting up and walking for the door.

Their father turned and stumbled, grabbing at the mantelpiece and knocking over a picture. It fell to the floor and they all heard the glass crack.

'He's had enough to drink, Mum,' said Richard, bending to retrieve the broken picture. He looked down at the photograph of himself. He remembered the day he'd had it taken in Aldershot; the whole sub-section had gone down in their uniforms and stood in line. The photographer could have retired on that day's proceeds alone, he thought.

'Enough, you say? Who are you to tell me what I should do, you little git.' He lurched forward and swung a big fist, knocking the picture from Richard's hand, and crashing into Richard, sending him backwards. Their mother screamed, and Richard scrambled to his feet as his father stood over him, his fists bunched.

'Calm down, Dad. You've had one too many tonight. Why don't you go and sleep it off, eh?' Richard squared up, lifted his chin and stared into his father's bloodshot eyes.

Their father stepped forwards and shot out his left fist, but Richard turned his head to one side.

'Stop it!' said their mother. 'For God's sake ...'

He twisted his hip, and then drove his right arm forward and Richard hadn't recovered from avoiding the last blow, and his father's fist struck him in the stomach below the sternum. He groaned, and his head came forwards.

His father grinned and lifted his left fist into his son's unprotected face. Richard's head snapped back, and he tried to bring up his hands to ward off the next punch, but his father grabbed his tunic collar and pulled him close, bringing his head onto Richard's nose.

The crunch of cartilage was audible even to Harry, and the boy came to his feet and stepped towards the fire.

The blood spurted from Richard's nostrils and he felt weak, his knees sagging. He looked at his father, saw him draw back his right leg, and Richard closed his eyes.

Harry grasped a fire iron and swung it overarm. It struck his father on the head, and the fight left him immediately. He dropped to the rug as if he'd been a child's puppet suddenly discarded.

Richard swayed on his feet and then looked around him. His mother stood by the door, a hand to her mouth. Harry stood a few feet away, his arms by his side and, indistinct through his watering eyes, Richard saw the poker. He looked down at his father's body and then he realised what must have happened.

He dropped to his knees and turned his father over. The crown of his head was covered in blood, but Richard had seen enough head wounds to know that they were often worse than they looked. He felt for a pulse in his father's neck, hunting around for the carotid, but he couldn't locate it. He wiped his own face to clear his eyes of tears and tried again. No pulse, and so he leaned close to his father's face. He couldn't feel any breathing. He looked up at the others, still standing as they had been.

'He's dead.'

*

No one moved for what seemed an age. And then their mother stepped forward. 'You must both go. I'll deal with this.'

Richard shook his head. 'No, Mum, this is down to me. I made him angry.'

'I did it, Mum. I'll go to the Police and say that I did it,' said Harry. Tears began to run down his face. He looked at the fire iron, stared at the few drops of blood that stained the rug beneath its tip.

'Give me a hand, Harry,' said Richard. 'Come on.'

Harry wiped his eyes and then leaned the fire iron carefully back in its rack.

'Mum, clean the rug. Now.'

She nodded and headed for the kitchen.

'Grab his legs, Harry,' said Richard. He reached down and took hold of his father's jacket and waited until Harry took hold of his ankles. Then the two of them struggled under the weight of their father, and dragged him across the room towards the hall.

Their mother squeezed past them without looking at their shared load, a bowl of soapy water and a cloth in her hands. She knelt before the fire and began to rub at the rug, and then rinsed the cloth, making the water pink.

Richard turned around at the bottom of the stairs. 'Go up three steps and drop him, Harry,' he said, and the young boy did as he was told. And then Richard lowered his father's upper body.

'Get a beer from the larder. Open it and bring it here.' Richard glanced over to his mother who was busy wiping the blood and hair from the end of the fire iron. He looked at his father who lay face down on the floor, his legs lying up the bottom three steps.

Harry came back with the beer. 'Thanks,' said Richard, taking the bottle. He poured the beer onto his father's jacket and over the floor. Then he took the bottle by its neck and smashed it on the lowest step. He rolled his father and kicked some of the broken glass and beer beneath his body before lowering him again. 'There,' he said. 'How are you doing, Mum?'

She stood and came over. 'Done. What do we do now?'

'Tomorrow morning, early, you go to the neighbours and tell them that you found him like this when you came down in the morning. They all know he likes a drink. Then they'll likely get the Police along, but it looks like an accident. Nothing to worry about.'

'But I can't leave him there, just lying at the bottom of the stairs. It's not right.'

'You must, Mum. It has to look like an accident.'

'And what about me?' said Harry. 'I killed him.' His bottom lip began to tremble again.

'No, Harry, you didn't,' said Richard, putting out an arm to touch his brother's shoulder. 'He fell.'

'When the Police ask me, I shan't be able to tell them that. They'll see I'm lying.'

'No, they won't.'

Their mother looked at Richard. 'Why?'

'Because he's coming with me. I was never here, and you tell the Police that your youngest has gone to find work. He's old enough. It was just you and Dad here, and he got drunk and fell down the stairs.'

She looked at her youngest son, knew Richard was right, and then realised her dreams of a university education for him, of a life different from her own, were all gone; shattered by the selfish man lying dead at her feet.

'Harry – go and pack a small bag. You won't need much because the Army will provide your necessities.'

'But what am I going to do, Richard?'

'You still play that trumpet?'

Harry nodded.

'We always need buglers, Harry.'

*

They stood around the kitchen table where they had earlier shared a meal. Two hours later, and all had changed beyond recognition. Harry had on his winter coat, a small cardboard suitcase in his left hand. He looked at his mother and he tried not to cry, and she wrapped her arms around him.

Richard looked at her carefully and he could see a shadow on the side of her jaw that make up had failed to conceal, and suddenly he felt no guilt about his father. He pulled on his damp greatcoat. 'We have to go, Mum. We can catch the mail train if we're quick.'

She held her younger son at arms' length and smiled through her own tears. And then she nodded, and released him to his future. Harry turned only once as they crossed the yard to the back gate, but his mother had already closed the door, unable to watch him go.

The two of them walked down the lane towards Denmark Hill where they hoped to get a bus to Waterloo. Neither spoke. They were lucky, and Richard pulled Harry up on top, despite the cold drizzle. The brothers sat huddled at the front of the bus and stared without seeing at the London streets as they passed by.

After a few minutes, Harry broke the silence. 'What do you do in the artillery, Richard?'

'I'm a driver.'

'What does a driver do?'

17

'There are six horses in the team, in three pairs. I ride the left horse in the centre pair.'

'While the horses are pulling the gun?'

'Yes.'

'How big is the gun?'

Richard smiled. 'It's a thirteen pounder. That means the shell weighs thirteen pounds.'

'And you get to fire it. Beats maths homework any day.' Harry was silent again as he considered his change of circumstances. 'I'll be alright, won't I, Richard?'

'Course you will. You've got me to look after you, Harry.'

Harry nodded. 'Yes. We've got each other. We'll be fine.'

The bus clattered on up Camberwell New Road towards Kennington and towards their uncertain futures.

Two

Harry looked up at a sudden noise, lifting a hand to shield his eyes from the glare.

'Aeroplane,' said Major Allen. 'Probably a straggler from Dover. The sky was full of them during the last hour or so of the crossing. Did you see them, Thatcher?'

Harry shook his head. 'I was below with the horses, Sir,' he said, his filthy uniform testament to his statement.

'Impressive sight.' Allen nodded. 'The Royal Flying Corps will be the eyes if not the ears of the BEF, Thatcher. At least,' he said, turning to face Harry, 'that's what I've been told. Makes you wonder what they'll need us for, eh?'

Harry stared at the aircraft until his eyes watered and until it became a tiny, dark speck against the brilliant blue of the summer sky, and then was gone.

'Thatcher! Don't just stand there gawping, boy. Give a hand with the horses, you waste of space.'

Harry turned at the voice of Corporal Pike screaming across the quayside.

'Thatcher's assisting me with squadron business, Corporal,' said Major Allen, frowning.

Pike marched up and saluted his squadron officer. 'Of course, Sir. As you like, Sir,' he said in a voice that managed to convey his disapproval of the officer's casual authority.

Allen returned the salute and stared at Pike's face; a face that bore more than a passing resemblance to his aquatic namesake: eyes that bulged and never seemed to close and his lower jaw protruding from beneath his moustache, showing a row of uneven, discoloured teeth. Those eyes now flicked towards Harry every few moments as Pike stood stiffly at attention before the major. 'Go on, then, Thatcher, you'd better lend a hand,' said Allen.

'Thank you, Sir. Well get moving, boy, you heard the officer.'

Harry saluted and began to walk to the dockside where the horses were being lowered from the SS Winifredian, one of the ships requisitioned by the army to get the men of the hurriedly formed Cavalry Division to France.

'At the double, Thatcher,' said Pike, his voice carrying clear across half of Boulogne, and Harry began to run.

'You going somewhere, young Thatcher?' said Milligan.

'Corporal Pike said you could do with some help, Sergeant,' said Harry, panting. 'They bringing ours up yet?' He looked up as another horse was swung out over the side, supported by a canvas harness slung beneath his belly.

'Aye – that's one of ours,' said Milligan, his Belfast accent strong.

They watched as two of their section, Riley and Hardcastle, stepped back as the animal reached the ground and then closed on the frightened horse to calm him while they released him from the winch and then walked him to a line of horses standing further along the quay.

'Thatcher.'

'You're popular today.' Milligan indicated Lieutenant Archie Smith with a sideways movement of his head.

Harry looked over and spotted their lieutenant standing on the gangplank that led onto the lower deck of the ship. The tall, thin officer waved him over and Harry broke into a run. 'Sir?' he said, saluting.

'I need you to give me a hand with Dancer. He's overwrought by all … this.' Smith waved his arm around his head as the two of them walked up to the top deck.

'I'll do my best, Sir,' said Harry with as much enthusiasm as he could muster. His troop officer's mount was a well-known equine diva, fussing over everything from his food to the tightness of his girth.

'He likes you, Thatcher.'

Harry doubted that, but he nodded all the same. They arrived on deck just in time to see Dancer kicking out with his hind legs at two Navy deckhands who just managed to leap out of the way before they could be sent into the harbour. Trooper Thomson now held the big horse by his bridle alone and, as the two of them twirled around, the deck cleared. Dancer stopped trying to escape Thomson and stood still for a moment, his eyes wild. The two deckhands edged back towards him. Dancer's eyes rolled in his head as he caught sight of the two approaching men. Pulling free of Thomson, he reared up on his hind legs, his front legs slashing the air around Thomson's head.

'Steady, boy,' said Smith, but Harry noticed he didn't take a step closer to his unsettled horse. And then Smith turned to Harry. 'See what you can do, Thatcher.'

Harry watched as Thomson spread his legs and pulled to try to bring the animal's head down, but Dancer was too strong.

'Go on.' Smith put his hand on Harry's back and gave him a firm shove.

Harry walked around behind Thomson and the pirouetting Dancer. When he could see that Dancer had spotted him, he walked forwards a few small paces and stopped. The two deckhands stepped aside. 'Rather you than me, mate,' said one with evident relief he was to be spared further involvement.

Dancer came down onto all four legs and looked at Harry. Harry could see that the horse was sheeted with sweat, white and frothing at his flanks. He took a few more steps. Thomson sensed Harry's approach and turned his head to speak: 'He's mad, this one, so you'd best keep your distance, Thatcher. I don't want to have to write to your brother and explain your broken neck before we even get off the boat.'

'It's alright, Thomson, I know this horse. He's a bit highly strung, that's all.' He reached into his haversack and took out an apple and his pocket knife. Standing still a moment, he cut the apple in half and slipped the knife back into the small bag that hung at his waist. The horse stepped from side to side, but watched the half apples that Harry held out in his hands.

Harry took another few steps and Dancer lowered his head enough for Thomson to release the tension on his head rope. Another few steps, and the deckhands looked at one another, smiled, and then began to close on the horse from behind Harry. Thomson moved aside, and Harry lifted his left hand to the horse's muzzle.

Dancer blew softly out of his nose and stretched his neck towards the tempting treat, and Harry saw the head rope go slack. 'Good boy,' said Harry, and Dancer pulled back his upper lip in a horsey smile, ready to take the first half apple.

Then he spotted the two deckhands closing in on him once more. He pulled at the head rope and it came free from Thomson's big hands, burning the skin of his palms. Dancer reared up, and then his hooves came down and sent the first deckhand sprawling, his shoulder broken. And then the horse went from standing to a gallop in the space of a half second.

'No!' said Smith from his position by the companionway door. But nothing could stop Dancer now, and when he reached the side of the deck, he didn't hesitate. He jumped as if following foxhounds and cleared the four foot railings by eighteen inches.

Harry and Thomson reached the side of the ship in time to see Dancer disappear beneath the waves, only to come up a few moments later swimming in desperation for the harbour's mouth. Lieutenant Smith stood rooted to the spot by the companionway.

Leaning on the rail, Harry handed Thomson one half of the apple. Thomson nodded his thanks and the two munched in silence as they watched Dancer heading towards England; whether this was by chance or some incredible equine homing instinct, neither knew.

'Good blooming riddance,' said Thomson around a mouthful. 'But don't you let Smith know I said that,' and a moment later, the young lieutenant arrived at the rail and looked out, appalled.

'Well, what will we do, Thomson?'

'Do, Sir?'

'We must get him back. That thoroughbred cost me two thousand guineas.'

'Well, I'm not going in after him, Sir. And anyway,' said Thomson, pausing to toss his half an apple core into the sea, 'he's making good progress. He might beat us back to Blighty at that rate.'

The three of them stared out at the horse's head until it disappeared behind the stern of a troop ship coming into harbour, much to the amusement of the soldiers standing on the far ship's deck. Then Smith turned from the railing.

His eyes fell on the unfortunate seaman whose collar bone Dancer had broken. 'You blithering idiot!' He advanced on the man who still lay on his back on the wooden planking of the deck. Beyond a groan, the man made no response as his mate helped him to his feet and then below to the ship's surgeon.

Smith turned away. 'Carry on,' he said over his shoulder as he disappeared below to the junior officers' quarters to get his kit.

Thomson turned to face Harry. '*It's alright, Thomson, I know this horse.* Thanks for your help, Thatcher.'

Harry grinned, and then they laughed, but the memory of the unfortunate Dancer soured the moment, and Harry looked out to sea again. But Dancer was gone.

*

'I do think it's partly your fault, Thatcher,' said Smith.

'Yes, Sir.' Harry hesitated. 'Why don't you have my mount, Sir?

Smith considered. 'I've always ridden a grey, and your horse is a grey.'

'A horse is just a horse to me, Sir, and I'm sure Sergeant Arthurs can organise me a remount from the transport lines.'

'That's a thought. Alright, you've convinced me, Thatcher. You go and see Arthurs and get yourself sorted and

I'll take your Lucy.' He walked around Harry's horse and patted her flanks and murmured in her ears.

'She's an honest horse, Sir. You'll not be sorry,' said Harry, bending to unfasten the girth to remove his saddle.

'Williams!' said Smith, and a young trooper ran up. 'Fetch my gear and saddle this mare, there's a good chap.'

Williams grinned showing that his two front teeth were missing, and turned without speaking to run over to the equipment store that had been established on the dockside.

With his saddle over his left arm, Harry walked away. He turned back once to find that Lucy was watching him. He'd been with her all through the long months of training at Tidworth and out on Salisbury plain as he learnt his horsemanship. She'd never let him down, but now he'd be going to war on a horse from the transport lines; it might as well be a blooming donkey, he thought.

'Sergeant Arthurs?' Harry spotted the middle-aged transport sergeant standing beside one of his horses, a foreleg raised as he inspected the shoe. Satisfied, he lowered the leg and moved around the back to check the other shoes. 'Sergeant Arthurs?'

Arthurs looked up at his name and then continued his inspection. 'Yes?'

'Lieutenant Smith has sent me to see if you've a spare mount. His … went astray.'

Arthurs stood and stretched his back. 'I heard all about it, youngster.' He chuckled. 'Yes, I can find another horse for your lieutenant, lad. Won't be as pretty as Dancer, and it can't swim.' He laughed again and took Harry's arm. 'Come on.'

Arthurs directed Harry along the line of the transport horses. They stopped in front of a large, black draught horse with white socks on his enormous feet. 'This will suit Mr Smith, I reckon.'

'It's for me.' Harry looked up into the horse's eyes. He pricked his ears and watched Harry with apparent interest, which Harry decided was a good sign.

'Oh, well. You might need a hand climbing onto him, lad. But he'll see you alright – although I doubt he can keep up with the rest of the fancy horseflesh in your squadron.' Arthurs unfastened the head rope from an iron loop in the wall against which all the transport horses stood. 'Here,' he said, holding out the end of the rope.

Harry took the rope and clicking his tongue, he walked the horse forward and then, stopping a few yards on, he decided to saddle-up. Walking around the horse's left side, he almost had to throw the saddle up to get it onto the animal's back. He reached beneath and fastened the girth and then he lengthened the straps on his stirrup leathers.

He stood back, and then looked around for a mounting block or convenient step from which he could ascend the enormous horse. Seeing nothing, he slipped his left foot into the stirrup and then holding the reins and the saddle pommel, he hopped and pulled, trying to raise himself up. The horse whinnied and side-stepped just as Harry's right leg left the ground, and he overbalanced, sprawling onto the dusty quayside. The horse pulled back his top lip and whinnied again.

'His name is Bramble,' said Arthurs, laughing. 'But we just call him Bastard.'

Harry stood and dusted himself off before taking the reins once more and walking Bramble towards a distant flight of wooden steps that led up the side of a warehouse.

When he had finally managed to get onto Bramble's back, the horse was perfectly well behaved, and although he was nothing like Lucy, he would do. Harry squeezed his calves, and Bramble walked forwards with a steady gait. He could see the rest of the squadron were already mounted and moving off the quayside. He passed into the shadow cast by the Winifredian and then back out into the heat of the late afternoon sun.

'Glad you could join us, Thatcher,' said Pike.

'Nice horse, Thatcher,' said Thomson. 'Bit on the big side for you, though. He must be seventeen hands and probably just as wide!'

Harry nodded and looking past the others he could see Lieutenant Smith astride Lucy, chatting to Sergeant Milligan. 'Yes. My legs are already aching; it's like doing the splits.'

The six hundred horses and five hundred men of the regiment left the quayside and headed out along a road towards a rest camp. After a quarter of an hour, they had left the harbour behind and the regiment occupied a half mile of road that ran alongside a beach.

Staring out to sea, Thomson said: 'What's that?'

Harry looked across to the water's edge. A row of fishing boats was pulled up in a line above the high water mark. The glare from the sun behind them made him squint, but he saw something moving between the boats. 'A horse?' he said after a moment.

Thomson laughed. 'It's more than just a horse, Thatcher. It's Dancer.'

*

The fisherman shook his head again and muttered something before taking a small, clay pipe from his pocket. Major Allen looked at Harry. 'He says he caught the horse in his net and so it's part of his catch, Sir,' said Harry, struggling a bit with a real French accent. The Frenchman took his time relighting his pipe and then spoke again.

Harry nodded and then turned to the major. 'He says Mr Smith can buy him if he likes.'

Lieutenant Smith exploded with frustration: 'But he's my horse. He cost two thousand ...'

'Calm down, Lieutenant. Ask him how much, Thatcher.'

Dancer stood a few yards away, tied to a boat's prow with a tar stained bit of old rope, but he seemed none the worse for his maritime adventure.

Harry relayed the question and then the answer while Smith stood quivering with supressed rage, looking between the Frenchman and Dancer.

'I've no idea how much that is,' said Allen. 'Here, give him this.' Allen handed over a couple of gold sovereigns. The fisherman took them, smiling. He opened his mouth and pushing his fingers far back to find his remaining teeth, he bit each one in turn. He seemed satisfied it was real gold, and he turned and untied the rope from his boat and handed the end of it to Harry.

'*Merci*,' said Harry, and then Smith pushed past him and took the rope and led Dancer away up the shingle. The rest of the squadron stood on the road waiting for the transaction to be completed, and when Major Allen climbed into his saddle, they moved off.

The sound of an aircraft overhead, and Harry looked up. He was getting used to them, now. After a moment, he followed Smith up the beach. He found Lucy tied by her head rope to Bramble, the two of them cropping at the long grass that grew at the margin of the road.

He hesitated, but he was too tired to shift his saddle over, and so Thomson gave him a leg up onto Bramble, and then they joined onto the end of the column and continued the short distance to the rest camp.

Three

2nd Lieutenant Edward Carmichael pulled his goggles down and looked out over the side of his aircraft towards Hardman. He nodded, and Hardman took a hold of one of the propeller blades and, grunting with effort, he pulled downwards, forcing the engine around. Nothing, and Carmichael nodded again, and this time, Hardman's effort was rewarded: the engine coughed and then roared into life.

Immediately, the slip stream cooled the sweat on Carmichael's forehead. And then came the familiar, sweet smell of the castor oil; used to lubricate the Gnome rotary engine that powered the Avro 504, it hid the smell of the mown grass strip. Carmichael waited while Hardman stepped clear of the front of his aircraft. He adjusted the petrol regulator. The engine power increased and the aircraft began to inch forward.

Although Carmichael couldn't see around the front of the aircraft while it was on the ground, he knew that he was on the centre of the grass strip. The aircraft bumped and yawed from side to side as it accelerated, but Carmichael made small adjustments with the rudder without conscious thought. The plane bounced once, and then the controls became light in Carmichael's hands as the Avro found its natural element. He looked over his shoulder and, behind him, Lieutenant

Marshall in the second Avro of their little flight was taking to the air.

He looked down at his map, the hastily drawn pencil lines indicating the direction he was to take. Carmichael leaned out over the left side of the rear cockpit. He couldn't see much ahead because the lower wing blocked his vision, and so he turned to look down and slightly behind, studying the ground beneath the trailing edge of the wing. He referenced his map; the harbour on the coast to his left must be Calais.

Marshall's plane drew level and he waved at Carmichael, and then banked away to the right, towards the south.

Cloud was building high above and ahead. The horizon was hazy, making visibility poor. He didn't want to get lost, and so Carmichael decided to hug the coast as he flew north, passing first Dunkirk and then Ostend. After that, he would head inland and have a good look around. Because somewhere out there, and no one knew where, a million Germans marched through Belgium and on towards France. And Carmichael and Marshall must find them.

*

Harry wiped the sweat from his brow with his sleeve for the tenth time in as many minutes. His movements in the saddle disturbed the flies that had settled over Lucy and himself, and his ears rang with their incessant buzzing. He flapped them from his face, and Lucy swished her tail. Neither made much difference.

He turned and looked back down the column. The regiment was strung out over a distance of some twelve hundred yards. Thomson pointed up ahead. 'Village. Maybe we'll get a chance for a break?'

Turning forwards, Harry could see the village. Earlier in the day, he had hoped that they would stop for lunch, but lunchtime had come and gone. The afternoon passed without any sign of a rest. The Cavalry Division was moving from the coast towards the front, wherever that was, and they were moving fast.

'I could do with a blooming drink, never mind a break,' said Riley. At the mention of a drink, Harry reached for his water bottle. He tipped his head back and swallowed the last few mouthfuls of tepid water.

They were passing the first houses now; nothing more than single storey buildings either side of the dirt road. Up ahead, Harry could see a commotion around the horses of the leading squadron. The column came to a halt. Riley stood in his stirrups and tried to see what was happening.

'What's going on?' said Thomson.

'Dunno.'

Harry undid his tunic collar buttons, hoping no one would notice. They'd been allowed to let the brass go without polish, to discolour and dull – but they'd still be expected to have them fastened to the neck. Now that they weren't moving, the heat was claustrophobic, reflecting off the chalky road. Harry's hand went to his waist for his canteen, and then he remembered he'd just emptied it.

The column began to move, and Harry urged his horse from its stupor with his spurs. There were more houses now, and the locals crowded at the edge of the road to watch as the BEF rode past. A young girl caught Harry's eye. Blond hair hanging to her waist and eyes the colour of the cornflowers they had passed on the roadside. He smiled, but she turned away.

Thomson laughed. 'Nice one, Thatcher! You made an impression there.'

Harry frowned and looked the other way but, a moment later, a tug at his stirrup leather made him turn again. The girl with the blond hair smiled up at him, her teeth brilliant in her tanned face, and he grinned back. She held up a jar, and Harry took it. '*Cidre*,' she said. Harry pulled the cork and tipped the jar to his lips. Cool and delicious, and he would have finished the jar if Riley hadn't reached across to try to take it. 'Go on, then,' said Harry, and stretching out, he handed him the cider.

The girl still walked alongside their horses, and she leaned up, her lips puckered. Harry hesitated, but then he leaned down from the saddle, and their lips met and her hand came up around the back of his head. And then his cap was gone.

Riley choked. 'She had you there, matey,' he said, cider dripping from his nostrils.

Harry sat upright, but she had stepped back from the column, laughing. She slipped off the badge and then tossed the cap back to him. He caught it at arm's length and turned it over to look down at it.

'That's coming from your pay, Thatcher,' said Corporal Pike without turning round. 'But if you pass me that jar, I might just forget it happened.'

Harry leaned over and took the cider from Riley's outstretched arm. Pike moved his horse to the side of the column and waited a second for Harry to draw alongside. He took the bottle and then dug his heels to his horse's flanks, disappearing with the cider. Harry shared a look with Riley and Thomson, and then he shrugged. Looking back down the street, he saw the girl was still watching him.

'She was a beauty, Harry. I'd say a kiss from her was well worth a blooming cap badge,' said Riley.

Harry nodded and pulled the cap back onto his head. He waved at her. She waved back, and then they turned a bend in the road and she was gone.

*

Carmichael was lost. He couldn't identify any landmarks now that he had headed in from the coast, and the cloud base had come down making visibility a real problem. He wiped the moisture from his goggles with a rag from his pocket and then looked down at his map. He looked over the side again, and he thought he could see the sunlight sparkling off water. There it was again, and this time he was certain: a river, and a big one.

He reckoned he might be overhead the city of Gent. Assuming that was correct, he merely needed to head due west to locate the coast and then head down its length to find the airstrip beyond Calais. He banked the aircraft to the right, giving the plane a touch of rudder to help her around. On his westerly heading, he kept up his observation, but so far he'd seen nothing.

Maybe he'd be able to see something if he got lower? He reduced power and let the nose fall a little, and the Avro began to descend. Carmichael felt distinctly uneasy as the Avro began to slice through the cloud. He worried that the damp would affect the plugs and that he might lose power with nowhere to go but down. But the Gnome continued firing on all seven cylinders without a hiccup.

And then he was through the cloud. Carmichael looked around, trying to re-establish his bearings. He looked over his shoulder, and he was pretty confident that the city behind him was indeed Gent. Looking ahead in the distance, he could see what he now assumed to be Aalter. He glanced downwards just as he crossed a road heading roughly northwest. He saw faces look up at the sound of his passing. But it wasn't the German army.

The road was crowded with civilians, most on foot, but some lucky enough to have their possessions stacked onto carts being drawn by a horse or donkey. Carmichael scribbled a note onto his map and banked the plane onto a heading that matched that of the road and flew along searching for the head of the column. After ten minutes of flying, he still hadn't found its end.

He knew he hadn't much to report, but he also knew his fuel was getting low. He decided to take a risk and cut the corner, flying directly for where he hoped the airstrip was. If civilians were fleeing their homes with all they could carry, they were fleeing from someone. And that someone must be the Germans.

*

Major Shears lifted his field glasses to his eyes at the distant sound of an approaching plane. 'Another one coming in,' he said to his adjutant.

'One of ours, Sir?' said Captain Anderson.

Shears hesitated. 'Maybe.' The airfield near Calais was occupied by Squadrons 2, 3, 4 and 5 of the RFC, so it was difficult to be certain.

Anderson looked away from the approaching aircraft and watched the activity on the airfield. 'Looks like we're just about ready.'

Shears lowered his field glasses and glanced across the grass strip to where equipment only recently unloaded after their arrival in France was now being reloaded onto motor lorries for their journey south to Amiens. 'We've still got two chaps missing, Anderson.'

'This could be one of them, Sir.' The Avro passed low over the perimeter and settled onto the grass with hardly a bump. 'Nicely done.'

'Probably not Marshall, then,' said Shears, and Anderson grinned; Lieutenant Marshall had very little experience in the air, but the declaration of war had meant an early end to his flight training.

'Go and see who it is, Anderson, and give them the location of the new airstrip.'

Anderson saluted and ran towards the new arrival, parked up by the line of trees at the edge of the airfield.

Carmichael climbed down from the Avro and pulled off his goggles. He arched his back and stretched out his arms, bunching and unbunching his fists; it had been a long day.

'It *is* you, Carmichael,' said Anderson, approaching.

Carmichael turned. 'Yes, Sir.'

'Seen anything of Jerry, yet?'

'No, but civilians are streaming out of Gent. I was overhead an hour back, and a constant flow of folk along the road to Aalter.'

'No sign of the Germans, then?'

'None, but perhaps Marshall had more luck.'

'He's not back, yet.'

Carmichael turned and looked to the east. 'He headed inland earlier than me, and the visibility was pretty bad. He'll show up eventually, I expect.'

'Well, we might not be here anymore.'

Carmichael turned to face the captain. 'Oh?'

'We're to make for Amiens. The BEF are heading inland and we need to be where they are.'

Carmichael waited for the news he dreaded. The captain hesitated and then smiled. 'So, get yourself something to eat, and Hardman and his lads will get you refuelled before they leave,' said Anderson, waving an arm towards Carmichael's ground crew. 'And then you fly down to Amiens. We'll join you tomorrow morning, but you'll find some of the squadrons are already there.'

Carmichael looked around, and sure enough, there were far fewer planes on the apron than there had been that morning. He nodded. 'Yes, Sir.'

'And take Sergeant Corbett with you,' said Anderson, referring to Carmichael's observer. 'I'll get your report, such as it is, to GHQ.' Anderson turned and walked back towards the CO.

Carmichael looked over to Hardman. 'Get her refuelled, Private. I'm going to get a bite to eat. And where's Sergeant Corbett?'

Hardman thought for a moment and then shrugged. 'Sergeants' mess, Sir?'

'Well, go and find him and tell him we're off in thirty minutes.'

*

'Down here,' shouted Harry, turning in his saddle to look back, making sure Thomson was still with him. Harry leaned hard and with a touch of rein and leg contact, Lucy changed direction, off the main track and down one of the narrow lanes between the trees.

Harry stared ahead, and he glimpsed their quarry in the shadows at the edge of the lane. He gripped the borrowed lance tight in his hand, the nine foot ash stave couched beneath his elbow. He risked another look behind, and Thomson was still there, grinning, his sword out of its scabbard.

Looking forwards once more, the boar had disappeared. Harry reined in and turned his head, searching the shadows.

'There.' Thomson pointed with his sword arm, seeing the animal scurrying away beneath the undergrowth to their right.

'Have you got it?' came a voice, clear through the trees.

'No, Riley,' said Thomson. 'But it's coming your way.'

'Come on.' Harry dug his heels into Lucy's side, and she jumped forwards and began to canter down the lane. Looking to his right, Harry spotted a gap in the trees coming up and he touched his right spur to Lucy's flank and with the lightest movement on the reins, she turned into the opening. Slowing to a trot, Harry looked back over his shoulder to Thomson.

'Damn.' Thomson and his horse had shot past the narrow gap, and he turned further along the lane and made his way back.

'He's still coming your way, Hardcastle,' said Harry, spotting the boar a hundred yards away, making straight for the other two men. He urged Lucy on. She broke into a canter, and Harry had to trust her to choose a good route through the close-growing trees while he kept his eyes on the boar.

Harry and the boar broke through the treeline into the next lane at the same moment, but the animal was some fifty yards to his right. Harry looked past it and saw Hardcastle and Riley dismounted further along. Riley turned at the sudden noise, saw the boar and brought his rifle to his shoulder. He fired, and the boar squealed as the bullet slashed across his upper back, ricocheting off the shoulder blade to whistle past Harry's head.

'For Christ's sake!'

'Sorry, Thatcher,' said Riley, pulling back the rifle's bolt to eject the spent cartridge and driving the bolt forward to push another cartridge into the chamber. He squinted along his rifle's sights, but the boar had crashed back into the undergrowth on the far side of the lane, and he had no shot.

Thomson appeared and Harry looked across at him, and then he laughed.

'What?' said Thomson.

Harry leaned over and pulled a large twig, still with its leaves attached, from Thomson's tunic epaulet. He held it up for Thomson's examination. 'Well, you're smaller than me,' said Thomson, grinning back. 'I can't duck underneath every blooming branch.'

'I think Riley winged him.' Harry tossed the twig aside. 'The pig squealed.' He walked Lucy towards the point where the boar had disappeared, and then he dismounted, swinging his left leg over Lucy's head to jump down by her right shoulder. He held her reins, but he knew it wasn't necessary; she wouldn't go anywhere without him. He knelt and touched his finger to a leaf and then rubbed his fingertips together.

'Well?' said Riley, walking towards him.

'Blood.' Harry held his fingers up.

Riley nodded. 'I got him, Hardcastle.'

'You've wounded him,' said Thomson. 'He'll be really annoyed, now. He's not a domestic pig. We should be careful. I'll go round to the next lane and wait, and you three flush him out.'

Riley and Hardcastle began to push through the foliage on foot, following the bloody trail. Harry swung himself back up into his saddle and turned Lucy to face up the lane. 'I'll go this way around, Thomson.'

'Right.' Thomson clicked his tongue, and his horse wheeled about and the two took off at a canter. Harry and Lucy headed the other way. At the top of the lane where it joined the larger track, many of which bisected the forest, Harry found Riley and Hardcastle's mounts, tethered to a large oak. The two lifted their heads at his approach, but then continued happily cropping at some low-growing vegetation.

Harry went left and then urged Lucy to a gallop, wanting to get to the next lane before Thomson; he badly wanted to get the boar – to bring home the bacon! The next lane was no more than two hundred yards further, and when Harry spotted it, he hardly had to touch Lucy's flank and she flew around the bend. And there was the boar; a few hundred feet up the lane, standing. Harry pulled hard at Lucy's reins, and she stopped in a cloud of mud and dead leaves. The boar heard the commotion of Harry's arrival and turned its heavy head to look at him.

Harry could see the matted fur at the animal's shoulder, red and slick. He gripped his lance tight and brought his arm out so that he could drive it down into the boar as he passed. He licked his lips. His mouth was bone-dry. He nudged Lucy with his heels and she walked on, her ears forward. The boar did not move. Harry kept his eyes on those of his prey: small, dark eyes, close-set either side of a long, grey snout.

Still the boar didn't move, and the distance was now only a hundred feet. Harry was surprised at the size of the creature, and he reckoned it at three feet tall at the shoulder. Probably around two hundred pounds of solid muscle stood, barring his way.

Lucy stopped, and for the first time, the boar moved, pawing at the ground. It lifted its head high, and exposed two large tusks, protruding from its lower jaw. Harry squeezed Lucy with his legs, but she made no attempt to move, her ears now pressed close to her head. He squeezed her again and clicked his tongue. She took an uncertain step forward, and the boar screamed and then charged forwards. Lucy took one step back, and then another, but Harry kicked her hard. He knew he must drive the lance down into the boar with the combined weight of the charging horse and his right arm to kill it.

Lucy was having none of it, and she reared. Harry held on desperately, watching as the wounded boar closed the distance with incredible speed. Lucy tried to turn, but Harry yanked at the reins to bring her around, the bit pulling viciously at her mouth. She reared again, and Harry fell back, his boots coming from the stirrups. He crashed to the ground, the wind knocked from his lungs.

He lifted his head and looked down the lane, and the boar was almost on him. Its eyes were black, totally focused on him. Its head was down for the charge, but Harry remembered those tusks. He watched as Lucy, with nowhere to go, galloped towards the boar and leapt clean over its charging body. The boar didn't stop, sensing that the man was his enemy, the horse irrelevant.

Harry new he should reach for the lance and he turned to look for it. He saw it, a few feet away off to his left, but he couldn't summon the spirit to move. He just stared at the boar. The animal's snout came up, those tusks shining white, and wickedly sharp. Harry knew he would die, and he knew it would be painful, and yet still he couldn't move.

And then the boar crashed into him, over him. Harry expected to feel the tusks cutting, gouging and slashing at his body, but nothing happened. The boar was still. The crack of the Lee Enfield had been lost in the noise of the impact. Harry lay on his back staring at the treetops.

A few seconds passed, and then Thomson was looking down at him from his horse. 'Alright?' He smiled as he slipped his rifle back into the bucket on his saddle.

Harry groaned as he rolled over, pushing the enormous weight of the boar from his legs. 'I'm not sure,' he said, coming up onto his knees. 'I think so.'

Hardcastle came into the lane further up, followed by Riley.

'You alright, Thatcher?' said Hardcastle.

Harry stood and looked down at the boar. He saw the bullet wound in the back of the animal's head and looked up towards Thomson. 'Nice shooting.'

Thomson smiled. 'Come on, let's get him back to camp. There's enough there for the whole squadron.'

Harry stepped past Thomson and looked down the lane. He saw Lucy a few hundred feet away and began to hobble towards her. She looked up at his approach. 'And where were you, my trusty steed?'

Lucy whickered, and then a moment later, when he was standing in front of her, she pushed her nose against him and then whickered again. Harry laughed, and stroked her head with both his hands. 'You're forgiven,' he said and, then wincing as he did so, he pulled himself into the saddle. He rode back up the lane to where the others stood around their kill.

'Has anyone got any idea how we can get two hundred pounds of pork two miles through the forest on horseback?' said Thomson.

Hardcastle smiled. 'I have,' he said, and he pulled a huge knife from his haversack. 'Divide it into four.'

Thomson laughed, Riley and Hardcastle joining in; and then, despite painful ribs, so did Harry.

*

Harry walked the horses down towards a stream that ran along the edge of the clearing in which the squadron had set up camp. The smell of wood smoke, of cooking food, reminded Harry of Scouts when he'd been a boy. He smiled when he remembered the first time he had been to camp: shy and nervous, clinging to his big brother.

The horses bent their heads and began to drink. Harry walked upstream a little way and knelt to fill his water bottle. He took a few, long swallows and then refilled it before walking back to the horses.

'Alright, Thatcher?' said Thomson, coming from the horse lines.

'Yes. Just glad that heat's gone.'

Thomson stroked one of the horses before looking across to Harry. 'We're moving towards Mons tomorrow morning. I overhead Captain Embury and Sergeant Milligan talking.'

'Mons?'

'Belgium, apparently. That's not far; we're only just inside France here.'

He took out his pipe and began to push some tobacco into the bulb from a leather pouch, worn smooth and shiny with use. He slipped the tobacco back into his tunic pocket before pulling a box of Swan Vestas from his trousers. He struck one down the side of the box. The match flared, and he held the flame to the pipe's bulb and began puffing with vigour. He smoked in silence for a moment or two, and then looked across at Harry.

A cool breeze ruffled Harry's shirt and swept the pipe smoke upstream. He sniffed. A fruity fragrance, and it reminded him of his father's pipe tobacco.

'The Captain was saying that we've got the French on our right and we're to hold the line to their left. Stop Jerry from getting behind us.'

Harry thought about that; it made sense. With the BEF on the left of the line, their role was critical: to stop the Germans from turning their flank and then marching on Paris.

Thomson took the head ropes of a pair of horses and turned to walk back up to the horse lines. 'We're for an early start, Harry, so you should try to get some sleep.'

Harry watched him walk away. Tomorrow they would be heading north into Belgium, and he knew that the German Army were heading south; they would soon meet. He led the other horses back, saw to their forage and then went to get some supper. Pork for dinner!

Later, he lay looking up at the sky, the stars brilliant against the black of night. He turned over, pulling his blanket and greatcoat up to his chin. He stared over towards where he knew Thomson, Riley and Hardcastle lay sleeping. Within days, perhaps even tomorrow, two great armies would clash. He closed his eyes, but sleep eluded him.

Four

Thomson slipped a big handful of army biscuits into a muslin bag. He pulled the drawstring and then folded it in half before placing it onto a flat stone he'd found at the edge of the forest clearing.

He picked up his rifle and then standing over the stone, he ground the biscuits with the butt. Kneeling, he emptied some of the crumbled biscuit from the bag into each of the mess tins. Then he added a few chunks of fatty pork to each tin before placing them onto the fire. Using his fork, he stirred the contents of each tin for a few moments.

'I can't believe we're doing this. At Tidworth, we'd have been up before Major Allen with tunics like this,' said Harry.

'Yes, but we hardly want to ride into battle with gleaming buttons,' said Riley.

'I suppose not.'

'Breakfast's ready,' said Thomson.

'I'll get yours, Thatcher.' Riley wiped the soap from his chin and slipped his razor back into his haversack.

'Thanks.' Harry continued rubbing ash and dirt onto his tunic buttons. He'd already dealt with the metal on Lucy's tack.

'Here.'

'Cheers,' said Harry, taking the mess tin, his stomach growling at the smell of the pork. As he ate, he watched the activity in the camp. Men were washing, eating, smoking. He looked over towards the horses. They had their forage and some of the men were checking their gear, and more than a few were standing in a line to get the tips of their swords sharpened by the armourer.

He finished the last mouthful of breakfast and then, still chewing, he pushed his tunic off his knees and walked over to Thomson. 'Thanks for the breakfast,' he said.

Thomson looked up. 'You caught the animal, Thatcher, and so it's thanks to you.'

'I don't think being knocked off my horse and trampled by a wild pig counts as catching it.' He grinned.

Thomson laughed. 'Maybe not.'

Harry knelt and brushed a few handfuls of ash and dirt from the edge of the dying fire into a small heap. 'I've got to dull down my bugle, yet.'

'Yes, we don't want to dazzle Jerry with your gleaming brass work.' Thomson stood up and walked towards the horse lines, returning with a small shovel. 'See you in a minute,' he said, and disappeared towards the treeline.

Harry walked over to Lucy. She turned to watch him. 'Hello, girl.' He patted her neck. His saddle was propped on its cantle, pommel uppermost. He bent and retrieved his bugle and walked back over to the fire, and sitting down cross-legged, he began to work the ash and dirt into the metal with a scrap of cloth.

*

Carmichael and Corbett crossed the damp grass towards their waiting plane. They could see Hardman at work on the engine, priming it.

'Morning, Hardman,' said Carmichael, the smell of the petrol dripping from the engine cylinders very strong.

Hardman didn't bother to look round. 'I doubt you'll be going anywhere, Sir. Not with this mist.'

'The meteorology chap says it will clear shortly, Hardman.'

'Corporal Yates is only in meteorology because he can't do anything else, Sir.' Hardman pulled down on the propeller and moved another cylinder into reach. He dipped a large pipette into a can and squeezed a rubber bulb, drawing petrol into the tube. Then he inserted the tube end into the engine cylinder and squeezed the bulb before repeating the procedure for the next cylinder.

'Well, it looks like he's right,' said Carmichael, and Hardman looked up from the engine. Even as they watched, the mist began to fold back, and they could see further along the mown strip of grass.

'Lucky guess, Sir.' Hardman turned back to the engine priming.

Carmichael smiled and walked around the far side of the Avro to climb aboard. He settled himself in the rear cockpit while Sergeant Corbett waited at the wing root. When his officer was seated, Corbett stepped onto the lower wing.

'What are you bringing that thing for, Sergeant?' Carmichael pointed at the old hammer gun in Corbett's hand.

'My father's shotgun, Sir. For protection.' Corbett put the weapon into his cockpit before lifting a leg over its edge.

'Protection from what?'

'Germans, Sir.'

'Really?'

'You don't think Jerry's going to let us have the sky all to ourselves, do you, Sir?' Corbett wiggled his bottom into the wicker seat back. He raised himself slightly and pulled the long tails of his leather coat forwards, and then tried to get comfortable again.

'I hardly think that you and that ancient fowling piece are going to discourage any Germans we happen upon, Corbett.'

'Right you are, Sir.'

There was silence as Carmichael began to go through his checks, looking left and right to watch the ailerons as he operated the yoke between his knees. 'You got enough ammunition, Corbett?' said Carmichael after a further pause.

Corbett smiled and held aloft a canvas bag of shotgun shells. 'Plenty, Sir.'

'Good man.' Carmichael glanced back at the tail as he rocked the rudder bar with his feet. 'How are we doing, Hardman?'

'She's ready when you are, Sir.'

'Right. Then let's get this show on the road, eh?'

*

'What is that place, Embury?' Major Allen looked to his left.

'It should be Casteau, Sir,' said the captain, but he checked his map to be sure.

The two sat their horses at the edge of a Roman road that ran northeast from Mons to Soignies. The rest of Allen's squadron occupied a field to the east of the road.

'And up there?' Allen waved his hand to the right.

'Soignies, Sir. About five miles further up the road.'

Allen considered for a moment. He took out his field glasses and trained them up the road to where it passed through a copse, the road in deep shadow. He was nervous of advancing straight up the road; anything could be waiting for them. But he was aware that their job was to 'get touch' with the Germans; to find and engage them and get word back to Divisional HQ.

'Right, Embury. I want you to send a troop along the road. Lieutenant Smith's will do. Get the rest of the men to dismount in the copse opposite and be ready.'

'For what, Sir?'

'I've no idea, Captain.'

Embury nodded. He turned his mount with subtle pressure from his knees. 'Lieutenant Smith?'

'You're wanted, Sir,' said Sergeant Milligan.

Lieutenant Smith looked towards the road and spotted Embury trotting down towards them.

'Major Allen wants you to take a look along the road, Lieutenant,' said Embury, coming alongside the Smith's horse.

'Yes, Sir.' Smith turned to Milligan.

The sergeant nodded. 'Troop will advance along the road in two columns.'

Embury reversed his horse and Smith led his men up past the major.

'Keep your wits about you, Lieutenant,' said Allen.

'I will, Sir,' said Smith, passing onto the road. When the thirty men and horses of his command were behind him, he tapped his horse's flanks with his heels and began to trot up the centre of the road.

Harry trotted just behind his officer, with Sergeant Milligan at his side. The older man looked over towards the youngster. Harry was biting his lower lip, and Milligan could see the lad's knuckles were white where he gripped the reins.

'Doesn't seem to show any ill-effects from the swim he had.' Milligan pointed at Dancer.

Harry nodded, but didn't trust himself to speak.

'Yes, I thought we'd lost him that day,' said Milligan. 'I still think it's a shame we didn't.'

'I heard that, Sergeant,' said Smith.

Milligan raised his eyebrows, and Harry smiled.

They were approaching the copse and, with the trees growing right up to the roadside, Smith couldn't see what lay ahead. He raised his hand and stopped. He stared up ahead, trying to discern shapes that might be hiding within the dark shadows.

Without turning, he spoke over his shoulder. 'When we get to the wood up ahead, I want half the troop dismounted to provide covering fire. Hold the horses this side. Then the rest of us will continue through the trees. If it's all clear beyond, you can rejoin us, Sergeant.'

'Yes, Sir,' said Milligan.

'I'll take Corporal Jones and Corporal Pike's sections.'

Milligan turned to organise the men.

'You're with me, Thatcher.'

'Yes, Sir,' said Harry, managing to find his voice.

Major Allen watched the two rear sections of Smith's troop dismount and begin to advance on foot either side of the road. He nodded with satisfaction; a sensible precaution.

When the two sections reached the wood, they began to push on through the trees at the margin of the road and Smith turned to face the remaining mounted men of his command. He nodded, and then began to trot towards the wood.

Harry rode beside the lieutenant and he stared ahead, searching for a hidden enemy. For the first time since arriving in France, it no longer seemed like an adventure.

They passed into the shadows, but Harry's young eyes adjusted to the relative gloom quickly. The road ran straight ahead and, unless enemy horsemen were hiding in the trees, the way was clear. They passed back into brilliant sunshine within moments, and Harry let out a long sigh of breath. They continued for a few hundred yards and then Smith reined in. 'Corporal Pike?'

'Sir?'

'Send a man back to the Major to report we're through the wood and then get the horses brought up for Sergeant Milligan's sections.'

Corporal Pike directed Riley back down the road and then turned to grin at Harry. 'Alright, Thatcher?'

'Yes, Corporal.'

Pike seemed about to say something more, but just then, Milligan appeared with his men from the trees.

'All clear, Sergeant?' said Smith.

'Yes, Sir. But…' He stopped speaking at the sound of hooves, and turning to look through the trees, he saw the rest of the squadron coming along the road towards them. He turned back to face Smith.

'You were saying, Sergeant?'

'Yes, Sir. We found signs of activity.'

'Activity?'

'Horses, Sir. And dismounted men. Someone has been in that wood, and recently.'

'Germans?'

Milligan shrugged. 'Hard to be sure, Sir, but given we're the furthest north of the cavalry screen, it's a fair bet to say it was Jerry.'

Smith turned to look back up the road. The Germans were close. Perhaps very close. Without thought, his hand reached for the sharkskin grip of his sword.

*

Corporal Yates of the meteorology section had been right; the mist had cleared and the heat of the previous day had already returned. Carmichael flew due north from the airfield at Maubeuge, their third flight of the day. Corbett studied his map, and looked down at the passing terrain. He could see British troops on many of the roads, but so far, no sign of the German army.

They reached Mons a little while later and crossed over the Mons-Condé canal that ran west to east before looping north around the town in an inverted U. Beyond Mons, the fields were full of stooks after the harvest, the crop cut close to the ground leaving only a golden stubble.

Up ahead, Corbett could see a village. Looking at his map, he knew it to be Soignies. They passed over a long, straight road that ran towards the village, and looking down over the leading edge of the lower wing, he saw mounted men advancing along the road. British cavalry, he decided, and he marked his map accordingly.

Carmichael had seen them, too, and he banked to the northeast, running parallel with the Roman road, now just off to their right. He could see the men looking up at them, trying to decide whether the aircraft was friendly. And then they were gone behind them and Corbett spotted a group of horsemen some distance away heading southwest along the same road. He turned to Carmichael and then pointed down. Carmichael nodded, and with a slight movement of the yoke, the aircraft descended to no more than fifty feet. They raced along, the road blurring as they passed, and up ahead, the advancing horsemen quickly took shape: Germans uhlans, with their lances and distinctive flat-topped helmets.

As they flashed overhead, Carmichael was sure he saw muzzle flashes as the horsemen fired their carbines up at them. Then a wooden splinter struck his cheek, and he saw a tear in the wing fabric as a bullet passed through it. He heaved left on the yoke, turning away from the road, and climbed for safety.

Heading north, they overflew Soignies. A larger force of the enemy cavalry was present at the edge of the town, and continuing beyond, Corbett saw field-grey figures advancing across the fields; thousands of them. He scribbled the approximate numbers and their direction.

After five minutes circling overhead, Carmichael banked to their right and gave the Avro a touch of rudder to bring her nose around more quickly. Heading back the way they had come, the Avro crossed the Roman road, and Corbett saw that the enemy cavalry screen had closed the gap with the advancing British cavalry south of Soignies. He realised that they couldn't see one another yet because of a slight rise in the road, but they were no more than a half mile apart. Corbett waved his arms and then pointed back up the road, but he had no idea if they'd seen him. But it wasn't his concern; they'd found the German army, and they now had to get word to GHQ.

Five

Harry looked up. He was sure it was the same aircraft that had passed over them earlier, heading the other way. He could see the two men on board looking down and the man in front seemed to be waving. He lifted his own arm to wave back.

'Friend of yours?' said Pike, riding behind Harry at the head of his section.

Harry didn't answer.

'I asked you a question, Thatcher.'

'No, Corporal,' said Harry, without looking round.

'Keep your arms still, then, boy. Stop waving them around like a blooming windmill.'

'Yes, Corporal.'

'What are you grinning at, Riley?' Pike turned his attention onto one of his other men.

'Nothing, Corporal.'

'A village idiot grins at nothing, Riley. Are you a village idiot?'

'No, Corporal.'

Pike was about to say something else when Major Allen held up a hand. 'What's that up yonder, Embury?'

The captain strained his eyes against the glare off the road. The heat was making the ground shimmer and distort, but he felt sure he could see movement. 'Not sure, Sir.'

Allen focused his field glasses on the crest of the road ahead. 'Damn this sun.' He tried to keep still, doing his best to ignore the attentions of the dozens of flies crawling over his face and cap.

'Uhlans, Sir,' said Lieutenant Smith from behind. 'I can see their lance tips glinting.'

'The benefits of young eyes, but I think you could be right, Smith,' said Allen. He waited as the distant figures came closer. 'I don't think they've seen us yet; I imagine we blend rather well with the background.'

'Permission to engage them, Sir?' said Smith.

'Embury, have the men dismount and take up positions perpendicular to the road, just in case we are seeing the vanguard of a larger force.'

The captain nodded.

'Lieutenant?'

Smith leaned forward in his saddle. 'Sir?'

'Take your men along the road and see if you can find out what's beyond that crest.'

'Yes, Sir.'

'And Smith, try and bring back one of those men alive.'

'Yes, Sir.' Smith turned to his section leaders. 'Right, lads. Let's go and give Jerry a surprise, eh? Thatcher?'

'Sir?'

'You ride next to me in case I need you to sound the charge.'

Harry nodded. He felt a moment of panic and had to close his eyes to prevent himself from simply riding in the opposite direction.

'It'll be alright, Harry.' Thomson urged his horse closer to Lucy.

Harry gave Thomson a thin smile, and then he and Lieutenant Smith began to trot up the road, the rest of the troop in column of twos behind them.

As they drew close to the crest, the enemy horsemen became more defined. Harry even thought he could see one man smoking a cigar. But they were certainly uhlans, he thought.

The Germans had cleared the brow of the low hill before they saw the British dragoons, and then they stopped, presumably to try to identify the approaching column. Harry watched as two of the distant horsemen conferred, and then they wheeled around and began to gallop back along the road.

'Line abreast!' said Smith, and the men at the rear of the column cantered forward and outwards to take up their positions at the ends of the line.

Smith reached for his sword, closing his hand over the silver wire-wrapped grip. He withdrew the gleaming thirty five inch, straight blade. He had had the armourer sharpen both edges of the last twelve inches of the blade, because Smith's father, a veteran of the South African campaign, maintained that: 'when you get in amongst them, you will need to slash and hack.'

Holding his blade upright, Smith looked left and right. 'Sound the charge, Thatcher.' He lowered his sword, and without waiting for Harry to lift his bugle to his lips, he dug his heels into Dancer and the horse leapt forwards.

Harry licked his lips and then blew the charge, the notes loud and piercing above the cry of the men. Lucy, caught up in the excitement of the other horses, stretched out her neck as she began to gallop down the centre of the road. Harry looked to his left. Thomson and Riley were closest to him, and as he glanced the other way, Hardcastle grinned back. Harry blew the charge again, and then again.

They crested the summit of the rise in the road and ahead, the four German horsemen looked back. Outnumbered eight to one, they did not intend to stay and fight, but dug their spurs into their mounts and headed for the safety of Soignies.

The Germans had been riding hard across half of Europe since the beginning of August; forage was sometimes scarce, and their horses were not at their best; the British cavalry were gaining on them.

Harry thrilled to the chase, his teeth bared and his eyes wide. He knew they would catch the four horsemen. They began passing the occasional farmhouse as they got closer to Soignies. The Germans' lead had narrowed to a few hundred feet and within minutes, they would have them, thought Harry.

And then he saw the other horsemen. There were, maybe, twenty five – perhaps a half mile beyond the retreating Germans. The odds had just changed, and the four enemy horsemen knew it, slowing their retreat to a canter.

Smith held up his hand and reined in. 'Sergeant Milligan. Section 2. Dismounted action. Take up position in that house.' Smith panted with the exertion of the chase and of holding Dancer steady. He pointed to an imposing house, set well back from the road in its own grounds, a veranda running along the south side.

'Sir.' Milligan signalled Corporal Jones's section to follow. Harry watched as they dismounted, the horses being held by two men as their colleagues clambered over the low brick wall that surrounded the house and made their way into the soft fruit orchard that faced up the road.

The remaining British horsemen spread out. Smith released Dancer to a canter. Harry could hear the slosh of the water in his canteen, the thump of his sleeping blanket behind him, the shouts of the men either side of him. He looked up at the movement of a curtain in the corner of his eye. It was a little girl watching their advance from a bedroom window in a house by the road.

'Sound the charge!'

Harry brought the bugle to his lips and blew, clear and bright. Twenty two blades came down in unison, but the Germans were no longer running. They had turned to face their pursuers, and with their numbers roughly equal, it would be a close fight.

Harry panicked; it was madness to charge at the enemy. He pulled at Lucy's reins, trying to slow her, but she ignored him, wanting to stay with the other horses. He pulled harder, the bit sawing in her mouth, and the other men of the troop began to edge ahead. Now they trailed some ten yards behind the others, but then the two groups of horsemen came together with a clash of metal and wood.

*

Carmichael brought the Avro in close over the perimeter and held the stick back until the point of the stall before letting her settle onto the grass strip. The plane slowed and came to a stop within two hundred feet, and as Carmichael pulled off his gloves and lifted his goggles from his tired eyes, he could see Hardman and the others on their way over.

'Alright, Sir?' said Hardman when Carmichael jumped down.

'Fine.'

'You found Jerry, then, Sir?' Hardman poked his finger through the torn fabric of the lower, left wing and then ran his hand down the leading edge spar where a bullet had torn off a piece of wood the size of a walnut.

'We found them, alright,' said Corbett. 'They're heading for Mons on the Belgian border. Tens of thousands of the beggars.'

Hardman nodded. 'We'll get her ready, Sir.' Already, a man was coming across with two cans of petrol ready to refuel the Avro. 'I'll have the carpenter take care of this,' he said, tapping the spar again.

'We'd better get along to the CO, Sir,' said Corbett.

The two of them left Hardman behind organising the repair and refuelling of their aircraft and headed over towards the cluster of bell tents that represented the headquarters of the four squadrons of the RFC that were occupying the field.

*

Smith was up in his stirrups like a jockey, his sword arm straight, his mouth open, shouting incoherently. The man he had singled out, the target he had chosen from a hundred yards away, saw the tall young British officer on his big grey bearing down on him. His lance was at the ready, but as the two horses came together, Smith sheered away to pass down the right of his target.

The sword went past the point of the lance, and the rest was easy. The blade struck the man in his chest with the combined force of man and horse at full gallop, and fully twelve inches of the blade showed in his back for an instant before he was knocked from his mount.

And then Corporal Jones's men began shooting. The British cavalryman is trained to fight on foot with his rifle, and marksmanship is as prized in the mounted arm as it is in the infantry. Years of live firing practice on the army ranges began to tell immediately. Harry watched a man topple from his horse, his foot caught in the stirrup. His frightened mount continued to canter forwards, dragging the wounded man, his head banging on the rough ground at the edge of the road. Another bullet took an uhlan through the head, his leather headgear flying from his shattered skull as he slipped from his horse.

Despite having slowed, Harry still found himself right in the middle of the fight. A German lancer charged him, and Harry's sword arm wavered as he tried to lock his elbow for the impact. The German grinned, realising the inexperienced boy would be an easy kill, and he rose up from his saddle, ready to drive the lance point through the British horseman. Harry froze, his sword tip not even pointing at his enemy. He felt the same fear he had had when the wild boar had charged him: he was unable to move. The uhlan was almost on him.

And then Thomson was there, his horse careering into the uhlan, knocking him sideways. The lance tip rose as the man sought to stay in his saddle, but Thomson's blade found its mark, and blood sheeted over Harry's face as six inches of sharpened Sheffield steel pierced the German's throat. And then Thomson was gone, turning his horse. Lucy, sensing her master's uncertainty, began to trot away from the butchery, and by the time Harry recovered, they were standing at the side of the road, watching the others fight.

Smith was past, the blade coming free from the dying German, and he found himself beyond the mêlée. Dancer turned in his own length, seemingly of his own volition, and Smith spurred forwards, coming at the Germans from behind. This time, he knew he lacked the shock of the full gallop, and so choosing his man, he brought his sword arm up to his face before swinging the blade in an arc that ended at the back of a man's neck. The steel hacked into the muscle and sinew, almost decapitating the uhlan, and he fell forwards over his horse's head, the blood a sudden, dark curtain. Smith drove Dancer into the scrimmage, and it was obvious that the sword was a better weapon than the lance once the horsemen were at close quarters. Within a few moments, the enemy cavalry were turning for Soignies and riding as if the devil were at their heels, seeking the sanctuary of their army.

Sergeant Milligan and Corporal Jones's men, somehow forgotten during the swordfight, now opened a fusillade at the departing uhlans. Another man was hit, but he managed to keep his seat, and the defeated German cavalry made good their escape.

Four men lay dead on the ground, their horses standing nearby, cropping at the long grass that grew at the side of the road. Smith's second victim hung over his horse's neck, flies crawling in his hideous neck wound. His horse's shoulder was black with his drying blood.

Thomson and Riley had cornered two of the German horsemen at the points of their swords. The two uhlans watched their comrades ride away.

'Well done, Thomson,' said Smith, breathless. 'Well done, lads. We showed them, eh?'

His men chorused their approval. 'Right. We must get back to the Squadron. Bring those two prisoners, Thomson.'

'Sir.'

'What shall we do about the dead 'uns, Sir?'

'Leave them, Corporal. The Germans can sort it out. Bring their horses, though. We could always do with remounts.' He paused. 'Mind you, they're not much to look at. Thatcher, you bring them along.'

The men began sheathing their swords, and turning back towards Casteau and the rest of the Squadron. Thomson patted one of the German horsemen with the flat of his blade, and the two uhlans turned with their escort and began to walk back under guard.

Harry dismounted and walked to the first of the German horses. A dead man lay beside the horse, his foot still in the left stirrup. Harry spoke in a soothing tone and then took the reins of the animal, patting its neck to reassure it. Then, without looking at the dead man's face, he took hold of his boot and pushed it free from the stirrup.

He took Lucy's head rope, and after tying one end to the uhlan's horse, he was fastening the other to a buckle on Lucy's saddle when Pike came over. The corporal stopped his horse next to a man lying on his back in the centre of the road, a little further away from the others.

Harry watched while Pike slipped his feet from his stirrups and jumped down. And then he saw the reason for Pike's interest: the man's hand had moved; he wasn't dead. Harry opened his mouth to shout out to Lieutenant Smith that they had a wounded man to attend to. Before the words reached his lips, Pike had pressed his sword onto the man's throat, sawing back and forth. The blade sliced through the gristle and bone in moments. Pike stood, his arms and tunic front soaked with blood. He wiped the sword blade on the dead man's uniform and then walked over towards Harry.

'Not as easy spearing uhlans as it is pigs, eh, Thatcher?' said Pike, sneering. He pushed his left foot into a stirrup and pulled himself easily back into the saddle, turning his horse to follow the others.

Harry looked over to the dead German and felt his stomach heave. He couldn't help himself, and he dropped to his knees and brought up the pork and biscuit from breakfast. Pike looked back and laughed.

Harry wiped the spit from his lips and taking his water bottle, he drained it in a few swallows. Feeling slightly better, and making sure he did not look down at any of the dead men, he finished securing the last of the German horses and then mounted Lucy. She needed no direction, and began to trot after the others, the four German horses tethered behind her.

Milligan and his men were already mounted when the rest of the troop rode past. 'Nice shooting, Sergeant,' said Smith, nodding his head at Jones's men.

'Thank you, Sir.'

Lieutenant Archie Smith rode at the front of his troop, and unlike his men, he had not sheathed his sword, preferring to ride with it at the present, firmly upright, the top eighteen inches dark with enemy blood. He had bagged himself a brace of uhlans, and he wanted to be sure everyone knew it.

Six

Smith looked at his watch; after midnight. He looked back and could just make out the engineers working beneath the bridge a few hundred feet away. Periodically, it disappeared behind swirling mist and sheeting rain. He hugged his greatcoat around him. The bridge spanned the Mons-Condé canal, a manmade barrier that separated the British from the advancing German army.

With the French away on their right, the BEF took up position along the southern side of the canal holding the extreme left of the line. Facing them was a German force of over twice their size that had thundered through Belgium with scarce a halt in three weeks.

Harry turned his head in the direction of the noise of galloping horses on a metalled road. 'Here they come, Sir.'

Sergeant Milligan appeared out of the gloom, big as a mounted bear, galloping hard along the canal bank. Behind him, Harry saw Thomson and Hardcastle. The hollow echo of the horses' hooves caused the engineers beneath the bridge to stop work, fearing they were about to be overrun.

Milligan passed the end of the bridge and brought his horse to a halt in a spray of mud. He dropped from the saddle and saluted to Smith. 'We've dealt with the other bridge, Sir.'

Smith returned Milligan's salute. 'Well done, Sergeant. Get along to Major Allen and let him know.'

Milligan nodded, remounted, and the three of them rode away from the canal.

'Right, young Thatcher, time to go.' Smith turned his back on the bridge and they began to walk after Milligan and the others.

'Any idea where the 1st Brigade is, Sir?'

'I'd guess they're back at either Élouges or Quievrain with the rest of the Cavalry Division.' He glanced at Harry. 'Your brother?'

'Yes, Sir. Haven't seen him since we left England.'

The two were quiet for a moment. 'Are they going to blow all the bridges, Sir?'

'Yes, but not yet; we'll be mounting patrols on the far side later this morning. Trying to determine just where the Germans are.'

Riley was waiting with their horses a few hundred yards further up the bank. Lucy pricked her ears when she recognised Harry coming from the darkness. He nodded his thanks to Riley and patted her neck. Slipping his boot into the stirrup, he climbed into the saddle, the wet leather soaking through his breeches. He turned Lucy, and then the three of them made their way back up towards Thulin, some two miles further south.

Dangling from ropes attached to the bridge, an engineer watched the three horsemen until the rain swallowed them up. Then he got back to placing the explosives at the foot of the bridge support. The quicker he could get it done, he thought, the sooner he could get some breakfast.

*

The damp mist condensed on the exposed engine parts. Hardman worried about moisture penetrating into the cylinders, but there was nothing he could do about it. He turned to look across at the marquee that served as an officers' mess. Still no sign of Carmichael, but with the rain from earlier and now the mist, he wasn't going to be flying any time soon.

Standing on the wing root to the left of the cockpits, he busied himself with a chamois, wiping the water from the low windscreens. Jumping down, he stuffed the damp pigskin into a back overalls pocket and walked around the aircraft. Four spars on each side connected the upper and lower wings. Hardman ran his hands up and down each one as far as he could reach. He felt the roughness under his palm when his hand touched the bullet strike from earlier in the week. He examined the damaged and repaired area, and he could see the carpenter had done a good job.

He repeated his examination of the other wing and then turned his attention to the cable stays. Finally, satisfied, he walked to the rear of the Avro, halfway along the fuselage where the cables from the yoke connected to the elevators. He ran his finger along each cable to check for any fraying. He walked around the rear and checked the right hand side before moving to the cockpit again. He was just examining a hole through the woodwork between the two cockpits when a voice interrupted him.

'Everything alright, Hardman?'

It was Carmichael. 'Yes, Sir. Just giving it a quick check. Another hole, Sir. You must be getting too close to the beggars, Sir.'

'Best way to see who they are, Hardman.'

'I'll get the carpenter to sort it. With this mist, you won't be going anywhere soon.'

Carmichael smiled. 'I'm just back from a visit with Corporal Yates.'

'Oh, yes, Sir?'

'He tells me the mist will burn off within the next quarter of an hour.'

Hardman stood and stretched his back. 'Right. Well, I've just got time for some breakfast, then. But I'll still have a word with the carpenter in case Yates is talking crap.'

Carmichael laughed as Hardman walked over to the edge of the field where the mechanics and other tradesmen essential to the maintenance of aircraft in the line had set up. Then he climbed onto the aircraft and looked for the hole. He pushed his finger through it and then leaning over the padded edge of the cockpit, he looked down and spotted the corresponding hole in the bottom of the aircraft. It seemed as if the bullet had gone between his legs before passing harmlessly out of the top of the fuselage between he and Corbett. It must have missed the upper wing because there was no tear in the doped fabric covering.

Carmichael jumped down and decided he would get a cup of tea from the mess while he waited for Yates's prophecy to come true. As he walked across the wet grass, he looked down. His hands were shaking.

*

Major Allen stared at the canal through his field glasses. The end of a bridge came into focus; a squadron of British lancers were approaching it from the far side of the canal. Lifting his glasses beyond the galloping greys, Allen spotted

German cavalry leaving the wooded area north of Mons and coming down the road in pursuit of the lancers.

The first of the British horsemen were over the bridge and cantering up the canal bank to the safety of the British lines. The lead horsemen dismounted and Allen could see the designated horse-holders gather the mounts while the rest of the men took up position for dismounted action.

As the last of the squadron crossed the bridge, the Germans arrived on the far bank. They showed no desire to cross in the face of the British rifle fire, and after a moment, they turned and retraced their steps to get out of range. One of their number lay on the ground, his horse gone after the others.

Allen turned to Captain Embury. 'It's not them. But it's getting hot down there, Embury; that's the second squadron across in the last ten minutes.' He bit his lip. On their earlier reconnaissance, he had sent Smith's troop to scout ahead, and when they hadn't come back, he and the rest of the squadron had had no option than to return to Mons without them before they were all cut off.

'There's nothing you can do, Sir.' Embury focused his own field glasses at the town of Mons, off to their right. He was too far to make out any detail, but he knew that the British infantry were moving through the town, taking over buildings that overlooked the canal that bulged around the town. When the Germans came, they would be able to fire on all three sides of the town.

'You're right, Embury, I know. But still, I can't return to Brigade without them. You get back to reserve and I'll hang on here.' Their regiment was part of the 2nd Cavalry Brigade and with the rest of the Cavalry Division several miles to the rear, they were the mobile reserve – to be called upon to gallop and provide fire-support wherever the need arose.

'Yes, Sir.' Embury slipped his field glasses back into their brown leather case and turned his horse. 'I'll report to Brigade.'

Allen nodded without watching as Embury rode off with the rest of the squadron. He lifted his field glasses to his eyes once more and stared across at the bridge.

*

Yates was losing his touch, and it was several hours before Carmichael and Corbett got aloft. They were flying north of Mons, and Corbett was scribbling onto a notepad, marking the disposition of enemy troops and their direction of march.

Flashing over the top of a small copse of trees, Corbett spotted a group of horsemen in khaki uniforms hiding to the south of the trees. He turned in his seat, and looking at Carmichael, he pointed downwards. Carmichael looked over the side of the plane and saw the friendly cavalry. He banked the aircraft to the right, a long, gentle turn that would bring them in a lazy circle around the copse.

Harry looked up at the sound of the engine. Although the aircraft carried no markings, he recognised the shape as being British. He waved up at the plane.

'Put your blooming arm down, boy,' said Pike. 'Don't you go attracting the attention of Jerry, you idiot.'

'It's a British plane, Corporal,' said Harry, but he dropped his arm nonetheless. In truth, there had been very few German aircraft since they'd arrived in France, but doubtless that would change.

Pike frowned up at the Avro. British or German, he didn't see it would help if the wretched thing circled over them. Bound to attract the attention of the enemy. He glared at Harry who turned away and busied himself with adjusting his already perfectly adjusted stirrup leathers.

Smith looked back at his map. He reckoned they were a few miles north of Mons. They'd been forced from the road by a large German cavalry force and had become separated from the rest of the squadron.

Milligan watched his officer fold and unfold his map while he tried to decide what to do. Milligan knew that so long as they went undiscovered, they were safe. But the longer they waited, the more certain was their capture. He glanced up at the circling plane which showed no signs of departing. Like Pike, he knew that it couldn't do them any good.

Corbett looked north and saw a large enemy force advancing through the fields either side of the road from Casteau to Mons. Looking south, now emerging from beneath the right wing tip, he realised that the way to Mons was relatively clear of enemy troops – if the British went now. He tore a page from his notebook and scribbled a rough map that showed the position of the enemy relative to the small British force. He also sketched a route plan to Mons and then added few words at the bottom.

Folding the note, he hesitated, wondering how he could safely deliver the message. After a moment, he leaned forward and removed his left boot. Slipping the note inside, he turned to Carmichael and then pointed at the British cavalry.

Carmichael nodded, and then increased the rate of turn, the plane momentarily passing the vertical as he rolled down onto the copse. They passed overhead no more than ten feet above the treeline and Corbett reached out and dropped his boot into the slipstream. He had the satisfaction of seeing it head straight for the British horsemen and then they were gone, Carmichael pulling the yoke in tight to his chest to climb.

The boot struck Pike on the back of his head knocking his hat off. 'What the…,' he said, spluttering with rage. He turned to see who had hit him, but the surprised looks on his men's faces told him they didn't know anything about it. 'Riley, get my cap,' he said, rubbing the back of his neck.

The boot had bounced after hitting Pike and landed a few yards in front of Smith. It took him a moment to realise what it was: a British army issue boot. 'Thatcher, could you pass me that … item of footwear?' said Smith, trying to maintain his composure.

'Sir.' Harry jumped down from Lucy. He bent and picked up the boot, and the message fell out. He paused and picked up the piece of paper. He handed both the boot and Corbett's notepaper up to his lieutenant before mounting Lucy. He made the mistake of looking over at a grinning Hardcastle, and he had to stifle a giggle. Pike was just putting his service cap back on. Someone laughed, and he glared around for the culprit, but everyone had a straight face.

Smith rested the boot on his saddle and unfolded the paper. He looked at it for a moment, and then handed it to a curious but silent Milligan. The sergeant studied the sketch and the two words at the bottom.

'Go now,' said Smith.

Milligan nodded.

Smith turned to his men. 'When we go, stop at nothing. Ride south to Mons. Get across the canal and find Major Allen.' With that, he dropped the boot, drew his sword, and resting its blade across the pommel, he urged Dancer to a trot, leaving the cover of the trees. Harry followed, close behind, and then the rest of the troop, with Sergeant Milligan bringing up the rear.

From a thousand feet above, Corbett watched them go, but it was then that he spotted the German cavalry emerging from a wooded area onto the road to Mons. The road onto which Smith and his men had just cantered.

*

Smith came onto the road and looked to the north, up towards Casteau. He could see nothing to alarm him. Then he turned his head to face the south, towards Mons. The enemy cavalry were just visible a mile or so further on. Smith held up his hand and the troop stopped at the roadside.

Milligan edged forward until he stood immediately behind his officer. 'What do you want to do, Sir?'

'We have to get back. We can't stay north of the canal. There's an entire German army behind us, so we must go on.' He stared down the road at the enemy, his own horse in the shadows of the trees that lined the road. They didn't seem to be doing much, just standing on the road. 'Right, Sergeant, here's the plan. We'll trot down each side of the road in line, keeping to the treeline. As soon as they see us, we'll wave and keep cantering down the road. Maybe they'll think we're Germans?'

'What happens when they realise we're not, Sir?'

'We'll charge, crash through, and then onto Mons.'

'It's a few miles, Sir. The horses will tire.'

'So will theirs, Milligan. And I can't think of anything better.'

Milligan nodded. 'I'll lead two sections on the far side of the road, Sir.'

'Fine. Right, well, there's no point in dilly-dallying. Troop will advance in column.'

Milligan spurred forward with two sections, and Smith began to canter along the left side of the road. Harry, following his officer closely, gripped his bugle tight in his left hand.

*

Carmichael and Corbett flew along the length of the Mons Casteau road over the German cavalry that blocked Smith's escape. As they passed overhead, the Germans looked up, and Carmichael made a climbing turn to the left, hoping that the enemy eyes would follow them and give Smith and his men the opportunity to close the gap. They certainly had the enemy's attention because as Corbett looked back down at them, he saw something punch a hole through the stretched fabric of the lower wing. A bullet.

He turned to Carmichael and lifting his shotgun, he pointed back down at the Germans. Carmichael smiled, his teeth showing white against his oil-stained face. He nodded, and began to line up on the enemy troops.

Descending rapidly, the plane accelerated to almost ninety miles an hour, and the German cavalry turned to stare at the oncoming plane. Several of the men dismounted and began to fire up at the aircraft with their carbines. Corbett had his father's old gun over the plane's side and, as they flashed over the top of the troops, he squeezed the trigger. There was no time to see if he'd done any damage – they were already climbing hard, pressed into their seats by the centrifugal force of the turn.

One of the spars that connected the two wings shattered when a lucky bullet hit it. Carmichael couldn't feel any difference in the handling, and he decided to risk another pass, to give the British horsemen a chance. Completing the turn, he levelled off, and then began to dive back down. He could see that Corbett had closed the barrel of his shotgun and was leaning back over the cockpit edge in readiness.

*

Smith could see that the aircraft had distracted the enemy horsemen. He reckoned they'd closed the gap to about five hundred yards and still they hadn't been seen. But then he saw one of the lancers point in their direction. A few heads turned their way, and two of them seemed to be discussing the approaching cavalry. Smith knew that as soon as they saw they weren't carrying lances, the Germans would know they were British; all German cavalry carried lances.

The aircraft made another low-level pass, but this time, only a few of the Germans looked up; they were too interested in the horsemen coming up the road. Harry saw the moment they made up their minds, the lances coming up and the horses turning to face the threat. Smith didn't hesitate, but began to gallop down the road, his men spurring forward behind him. They didn't spread out. The intention was to cut through the enemy line and straight on down the road, no time for a fight.

Four hundred yards. Three fifty, and now the Germans knew there was an enemy patrol trying to get back to Mons. *Three hundred yards*. The lancers spread across the road, in two ranks, and began to canter towards the smaller, oncoming British force. *Two hundred and fifty yards*, and then the aircraft was so low overhead that Harry pressed his head against Lucy's shoulder. *Two hundred*. It continued past the galloping dragoons and straight at the advancing German lancers. Harry thought it would hit the ground, but somehow the pilot kept the aircraft just feet above the road, and flew straight at the enemy. *A hundred yards*.

The German horsemen scattered left and right, several riders falling from their mounts. *Fifty*. And then the aircraft was through and climbing, and Smith struck the leading enemy lancer with his sword, grunting with the effort, the blade coming free in a gush of blood and his column sliced the German line in half, swords clashing against the wooden shafts of the lances as they passed through.

By the time the enemy had turned their horses to give pursuit, they had a hundred yards on them. Harry didn't even look back, he just raked Lucy's sides with his spurs, pressed his head close to her long neck and prayed that they wouldn't be caught.

There came the light crack of the enemy carbines as some of the Germans tried to shoot the fleeing British, but the weapon lacked the range and accuracy of the British Lee Enfield rifle with which all British cavalry were equipped. Milligan, riding at the rear of the British column, looked over his shoulder and saw that they were opening the gap with the Germans, and for the first time since they had become separated from the rest of the squadron, he thought they might make it back to the British lines. The bullet, a lucky shot, struck him in his right shoulder, and his arm went numb. He let go of his sword, and it hung from its wrist strap, bouncing against his horse.

Lucy's ears were forward, and she tried to pass Dancer, the two of them almost neck and neck as they ran. Smith looked over and grinned at Harry, but Harry was too focussed on his fear to notice. He looked up, and in the distance he caught sight of Mons, the canal shining in the brilliant morning sun. Another horse came up level with Lucy and Dancer. Harry glanced over to his left: it was Agamemnon, Milligan's horse. But of Milligan there was no sign.

Up ahead, Harry watched British infantry standing up to see who was coming, and for a moment, he was certain they would be shot by their own side. But someone recognised the charging horses as British cavalry and the defenders held their fire. The hooves rang loud and hollow over a bridge, and then they were across, the troop slowing to canter up the canal bank and suddenly, a cacophony of small arms fire came from behind them; the infantry had seen the German lancers, and they opened up an intense rifle fire. One enemy horseman made straight for the bridge, his head low and his arm outstretched, the lance tip glinting. He was hit several times before he fell, and his horse slowed and then stopped on the British side of the canal. The other horsemen dismounted and began to shoot back across the narrow strip of water, but they had no cover, and the British rifles were too accurate. Within a few minutes, it was over, the Germans pulling back, and the canal fell quiet.

Smith, exhausted, slipped from his saddle and wiped his face with a handkerchief. He grinned up at his men, still mounted, and then he opened his water bottle with shaking hands and emptied it in a few quick swallows.

'Sir,' said Harry. 'It's Sergeant Milligan, Sir.'

'What about him, Thatcher?' Smith pushed his water bottle back into its webbing holder at his belt.

'He's not here, Sir.'

Smith froze, the bottle half in and half out of the webbing and looked up at Harry, with Milligan's big bay horse standing beside Lucy. He walked over, and there was blood on the saddle and the horse rug. He nodded. There was nothing to say. They'd suffered their first casualty, and he knew that there would be more before the day was over.

Seven

The rifle and machine-gun fire was continuous now, but muffled by the two miles distance that separated the 2nd Cavalry Brigade from the canal at Mons. Harry rubbed his hand across the back of his neck and winced. Sunburn, and he regretted not having done as Riley had and rolled down his service cap's neck cover. Every time he turned his head and the rough tunic cloth rubbed his skin, he was reminded of his own stupidity.

Using a hand to shield his eyes from the glare, as he watched, he saw the soil thrown up on the south side of the canal. He guessed that a German high-explosive shell was the culprit. Between the canal and where he stood, he spotted the railway line running past Thulin, and he knew that down there, somewhere, his brother, Richard, was waiting. The thump of the high-explosive shell now reached him on the low ridge, and Harry looked back towards the canal.

A messenger pulled up his horse in a cloud of dust, stopping just in front of Major Allen. 'From Division, Sir,' he said, handing Allen a note. Harry, no more than twenty yards distant, watched while the major unfolded the piece of paper and studied its contents. The messenger waited in case there was a reply, his horse's ears back and stepping from side to side.

Harry saw Allen shake his head. 'Nothing further.' The messenger hauled at his reins, turning his horse, and then took off back to Divisional HQ.

Allen turned in his saddle and looked for Captain Embury. 'We're to advance to within range of the canal, Captain. Providing supporting fire for the infantry.'

Harry slipped his foot into a stirrup and pulled himself into the saddle before taking up his bugle in readiness. Riley, Hardcastle and Thomson mounted their own horses, and then they waited the command to advance.

They crossed the railway line at the canter and on down the slight hill. As they came closer to the canal, so the noise of the battle increased. Harry found he was now able to distinguish the sounds of specific weapons: the chatter of a Vickers machine-gun; the crack of the Lee Enfield rifles as the infantry sent twenty rounds a minute across at the massing German troops; the sound of the field artillery pieces firing at point-blank range across the canal. Harry felt the stirrings of his fear in anticipation of the imminent action.

*

The German machine-gun poured fire onto the British troops, forcing them to keep their heads low.

'They've got it in the house opposite, Sir,' said a sergeant of the 1st Battalion Dorset Regiment, ducking his head back down as the bullets sliced the air around him.

His lieutenant nodded, and risked a look back across the canal. Thank God the bridge had been blown that morning by the cavalry, because he knew they couldn't hold them. The opposite bank was swarming with field-grey figures, and although his men were firing as fast as they could load a round into their rifle chambers and pull the trigger, it was not going to be enough. He knew that the Germans would have engineers; men who could span the ten foot gap in the middle of the bridge, and then the enemy would swarm across.

Even while he watched, he saw a small group of Germans attempting to swim across the canal to get to the controls of a swing bridge. His sergeant spotted them too, and despite the withering machine-gun fire, the sergeant knelt up and carefully took aim. His first shot struck the leading swimmer in the head; he slipped beneath the surface of the water without a sound. The sergeant reloaded, and then fired again, and a second man was hit. Their colleagues looked up at the British from the canal and thought better of it, returning to their own bank. The body of the first man floated where he'd died, the water pink around him. The sergeant reloaded, and then knelt back behind the wooden cart that served as a barricade.

The lieutenant turned at the sound of approaching horses. A few hundred yards behind them, a battery of horse artillery cantered up, and then the six teams turned, slewing their guns around to face the canal. The lieutenant watched as men unlimbered the guns and their ammunition wagons. Within moments, the first gun rocked back on its trails, and then almost instantly, the roar of the shell reached the lieutenant's ears. He turned his head, and saw the horrendous effect of the shrapnel on the massing enemy infantry. Then the remaining five guns of the battery fired, almost simultaneously, and the Germans fell back. But the machine-gunners in the house on the far bank turned their attention to the artillery, and enemy rounds began ricocheting off the metal shields of the guns behind which the British gunners crouched, loading, firing and loading again.

*

Having secured the horses to the picket pegs that each man carried as part of his kit, Harry squatted on his haunches in the shade cast by Lucy. Riley, Thomson and Hardcastle had run forward to help the infantry at the canal, and Harry was glad to be the nominated horse holder.

Not far away, he could see a battery of artillery, and he wondered whether Richard was there, behind the guns. Some of the men there had stripped to the waist, and he watched them for a while as they moved ceaselessly back and forth between the guns and their piles of ready ammunition.

He turned his head to look along the length of the canal, shining with reflected sunlight over by Mons. He found it hard to believe that they were unable to advance. Yesterday, they'd been chasing German cavalry patrols, and now they were fighting for the very existence of the BEF, the full weight of an entire German Army hammering at their small force.

The afternoon passed slowly, and much later, Fred Williams ambled over. He grinned down at Harry. 'Got anything to eat?' he said after a moment.

Harry shook his head. He'd eaten his rations earlier in the day, and now there was nothing until dinner. Whenever that would be.

'Cigarette?'

'Don't smoke, Williams.'

Williams looked down towards the canal. 'Looks like hot work, doesn't it?'

Harry didn't respond and, after a moment longer, Williams, still hungry, went on his way to see if he could scrounge anything from the others of the regiment still not engaged.

*

Thomson took careful aim, holding his breath at the instant that he took up the second pressure of the trigger. The bullet left the muzzle of the rifle at about 2,500 feet per second, and passed through the German corporal's head, killing him before the sound had time to catch it up. His men gawped down at his twitching body, and then scattered left and right, seeking cover.

Thomson worked the rifle bolt, ejecting the spent cartridge and forcing another into the chamber. He moved his rifle to the left, spotting another NCO, and again, he fired. The man spun around, clutching at his arm. The shot was low, and the German sergeant staggered back from the force of the bullet strike, but he would probably live.

Thomson had counted his shots in his head, and he reached for a clip from the leather bandolier he had laid beside him. He rolled onto his left side, aligned the cartridge charger with the grooves on his rifle and pushed the five rounds down into the magazine. He reached for a second charger, and repeated the action, and then rolling flat once more, he pushed the bolt forwards and lowered his eye to the rear rifle sight and began to search for another target.

Further along the canal, just north of the town of Mons, the Germans were trying to force a rail bridge that had not been destroyed. Nimy Bridge spanned the canal at the most northerly point of the sliver of water that separated the two armies. Lieutenant Dease, 4th Battalion, Royal Fusiliers, knelt behind his men on the southern end of the bridge. The number one of his machine-gun team pressed the firing button on the Vickers, and the German attack faltered as the rounds took their toll. Dease turned and reached back for another box of ammunition, and then a bullet struck him, sending him sprawling across the gravel bed beneath the tracks.

'You're hit, Sir,' said a private.

'I'm alright, Godley.'

Godley helped his lieutenant to his knees, and then the two of them dragged several boxes of ammunition forwards. Looking back across the bridge, Dease knew they couldn't hold on forever. But then they didn't have to. They just needed to give the rest of their battalion time to get away. The number two nodded his thanks to Dease and Godley, and then pulled a canvas belt of ammunition from the nearest box and made ready to feed it into the Vickers' breech.

The Germans had been waiting. When, a moment later, the Vickers fell silent as the team began reloading, they ran forwards, trying to cover the distance to the British machine-gun team. They got halfway across, and then just as the number one was about to press the firing button on the Vickers, a round shattered his skull, blood and soft grey matter splattering across Dease's tunic. His number two made to replace him, but the German rifle fire killed him, too.

'Godley!' said Dease, and the private dragged the two bodies clear and took up position behind the machine-gun. The enemy were only yards away, and Dease reached for his pistol. A bullet plucked at his tunic, another sliced through his service cap, parting his hair but missing his head, and then Godley began to fire. Dease watched the Germans fall, and it reminded him of skittles: they fell in a line as Godley traversed the gun, and within moments, the bridge was again empty of enemy troops. A breathing space, no more.

Off to the East, the Germans had already crossed over and were threatening the right flank, driving a wedge between the BEF and the French army. And far down to the left of the line, near Condé, where the canal made a right-angle turn to the south, the Germans were almost across. In a short while, they would be able to turn the British left flank, and like the horns of a bull, the Germans could encircle the BEF, trapping them; removing them from the war at a stroke. It was time to withdraw.

*

'Get them ready, Thatcher,' shouted Lieutenant Smith as he ran up the gentle slope towards the waiting horses. Harry stood and unfastened the horses from the picket pegs before pulling them from the ground and returning them to each horse's saddle next to the sword scabbard.

Thomson arrived first, panting hard. He grabbed the reins and was in his saddle. 'Come on, Thatcher. Get mounted, lad.' He looked back the way he had come. 'Come on!'

Harry, still holding the other two horses by the reins, pulled himself up onto Lucy's back. She turned her head and looked back at him, sensing the excitement; the imminence of action after an idle afternoon in the sun.

Riley and Hardcastle arrived, and Harry watched as Riley slotted his rifle into its bucket before mounting.

'Let's go.' Smith kicked his heels to Dancer's sides, and the big horse reared, and then the two were off, heading southwest, away from the canal, towards the river L'Escaut that provided a natural barrier to the west. The rest of the troop galloped after their officer, crossing the railway line they'd cantered over earlier during the day.

'How was it?' said Harry, looking across at Riley.

Riley shook his head. 'Bad. We can't hope to hold them.'

'What's happening now?'

'We're to move back, then we dismount and hold the Germans off while the infantry retire past us.'

Harry looked back over his shoulder towards the canal. He could see the battery of horse artillery had moved further south, away from the canal, but still engaged with the enemy. The sound of the guns was more muffled, now, but still a constant din. Ahead, a column of infantry was doubling along a road. Lieutenant Smith raised a hand, and the troop came to a stop.

'Take Dancer, Thatcher. Wait here.'

Harry jumped down and gathered the reins of his comrades' horses. Riley grabbed his rifle, pulling back the bolt to eject a cartridge. He stopped by his horse's neck to grab the spare bandolier of ammunition, and then he ran after the others towards the retreating infantry. Harry looked back towards Mons, and he couldn't spot the artillery. And then, a moment later, he saw them, beyond the railway tracks, on the move south, deploying into line once more. Within minutes, the sound of the guns carried to Harry as they engaged the advancing ranks of field-grey infantry.

And so it continued through the night: they would mount up, ride southwest for a short distance, and then redeploy to face the approaching Germans. Harry huddled with the horses, his fear nauseating. He wondered whether he would rather be in action himself, instead of an impotent spectator. Then, out of the night came small arms fire, a few shots at first, separate and distinct. Then a crescendo as each man shot repeatedly at the massing shadows.

When contact was made, the Germans sought cover, scraping shallow trenches from which to return fire. And before they could overwhelm the thin British cavalry screen, the horsemen had melted into the darkness to repeat the process a mile or so further on.

*

Carmichael looked down at the advancing German First Army. He and Corbett had been airborne since before dawn, and had been following the Germans' progress since they had found them, southwest of Mons. Flying further on, they found the British 5th Division. They had been chased fifteen miles by the advancing Germans, and Carmichael had found them near a village called Audregnies, still just inside Belgium. The rest of the British 5th Division and the Cavalry Division were spread across the flat ground between Quiévrechain to the west and Élouges some five miles to the east.

Corbett annotated his map, marking the troop dispositions. He knew that the Germans were advancing fast on the French Army, and that it was important that the British slow the Germans for as long as possible. He turned to face back and gave Carmichael a thumbs up. They had what they wanted.

*

'You got any of that pork left, Thatcher?' said Riley.

'No. And in any case, it would be pretty rank by now after the heat yesterday.'

'I'd eat the arse out of a camel right now.'

Thomson's stomach rumbled in agreement, and he smiled. 'Anyone got anything to eat?'

No one responded. 'Right,' Riley said. 'I'm going to make a brew.'

He opened his haversack and pushed his hand deep into the webbing, searching for his stash of tea leaves. Grinning, he brought them out in a little tobacco tin.

Harry knelt over a small stove, one they'd all helped buy and which he carried on his horse. He began pumping the oil in the reservoir to get the pressure up. Then he felt in his tunic pockets for matches.

'Here.' Thomson tossed a box down.

Harry turned on the fuel and when he heard a hiss, he struck a match, holding the flame to the nozzle. A moment later, the vapour ignited with a blue flame.

Riley shook some of his precious tea leaves into his mess tin and then emptied his water bottle over them. He handed the tin down to Harry, returning the tobacco tin with the remainder of the leaves to his haversack.

Hardcastle fetched his mess tin in expectation and Thomson produced an enamel cup.

'Where'd you get that?' said Harry.

'Been saving it for a special occasion.'

The water began to boil, so Harry turned off the oil supply. They had no strainer, so a he used a muslin bag. Harry was about to toss the soggy tea leaves away when Riley stopped him. 'It's going to be a long day. We might want those again.'

Harry nodded and laid the bag aside to cool. The four of them stood in silence, drinking their tea. The noise of an engine drew their eyes upwards, and Harry thought he could see an aircraft turning above them, beginning to head northeast.

'That was a hell of a long night,' said Thomson, his tea finished.

It was getting lighter, and the four looked north, the direction from which they knew the Germans would come. Already, they could see movement north of Quiévrain. Enemy artillery batteries had deployed on the far side of the railway line. And around them poured the entire German First Army, a hundred and sixty thousand men intent on destroying the BEF.

Off to their right, two great gouts of earth flew up, and no sooner had Thomson noticed them than the sound of the opening salvo reached them from across the plain. 'Here we go.' He tossed the dregs of his tea into the dry grass at his feet before walking back to his horse and tightening its girth strap.

*

Carmichael completed the gentle left turn and, glancing back over his shoulder at the British, he was suddenly glad he wasn't standing in the way of the German Army. The engine coughed and, instinctively, Carmichael reached for the petrol regulator, adjusting the mixture to settle the engine. It made no difference, and the engine began to run very rough, the plane sinking in the cold, dawn air. Corbett turned and looked at him. Carmichael shrugged, but carried on trying to get the engine to settle.

A rip appeared in the surface of the wing fabric above Corbett's head. He heard nothing but saw it blossom. And then a piece of wood was torn from the edge of the cockpit. It was only when a bullet passed through the wicker chair and into his thigh that he realised that the Germans were shooting up at them. Corbett looked down at his groin. A dark stain had already appeared, soaking his trousers. He knew it must be serious, and panic gripped him. He turned to look at Carmichael, but the pilot was still busy fighting with the engine. And even as Corbett turned back, the engine stopped.

Carmichael couldn't understand why the engine had packed in, but he knew he didn't have time to get it going again before they reached the ground. He had only one alternative, and so he began to look for a suitable landing site.

The ground was fairly flat, but here and there were roads, small villages and the occasional slag heap that sat near the shaft of a coal mine. At the back of his mind, Carmichael realised that if he managed to survive the landing, he would probably spend the war as a prisoner. He tapped Corbett on the shoulder. The man didn't respond. Carmichael had no time to worry about it, and instead turned onto finals, his landing site selected more by default than real choice.

The plane slowed as he pulled back the stick, and the aircraft began to settle towards the ground. It was still quite dark, and Carmichael hadn't seen the railway line that slashed across the plain. The railway line that was raised a couple of feet above the surrounding ground on a thick bed of gravel.

Eight

The undercarriage skid caught the gravel bed and tipped the aircraft onto its nose. The Avro went from thirty knots to zero in a few feet, pitching both Corbett and Carmichael forwards. Carmichael was thrown from the aircraft, landing some yards away. He lay, momentarily stunned, and rather surprised to be alive. He sat up, and then looked across at his plane.

The aircraft stood on its nose, its tail high in the air. Apart from the crushed engine cowling, it didn't look too bad. Carmichael could see Corbett hanging from the front cockpit. He stood and limped towards him.

'Corbett?' he said as he approached, but then the smell of petrol stopped him in his tracks. There was no response. 'Corbett?' Conquering his fear of fire, Carmichael edged closer. He reached the side of the plane and knelt next to the fuselage. He could see, now, that the wings were broken at the roots. He could also see that Corbett was dead. The sides of his cockpit were bathed in his blood and it dripped dark and thick onto the gravel. Carmichael leant in to check for a pulse to be sure. Nothing.

He heard voices, and he stood to look around the wreck. He could just make out figures in the dim light running towards him. He dropped low, hesitated, and then reached in past Corbett's body and grabbed his shotgun. Tugging it free, he looked into the cockpit for the shells. The canvas cartridge bag was stuck beneath the wicker seat. Carmichael stood, checked on the approaching Germans, and then ducked back down, stretched his arm and pulled at the bag's leather strap. He couldn't get it free, and then he detected an electrical smell. The contact breakers were still closed, and all it would need was a spark. He gave the bag one last almighty tug, and at last, it came away from between the seat and the cockpit.

He stood, holding the weapon in one hand, the bag by its strap in the other. He risked another quick look at the advancing infantry, and then he hobbled away from the aircraft towards the silhouette of a building. He had gone no more than twenty yards when he was knocked to the ground. A blast of hot gas enveloped him, the concussion squeezing the air from his lungs. Then the sound of the explosion came. The Avro's fuel had ignited, and the plane had gone up instantly.

He rolled onto his face and turned to look back and, sure enough, a half a dozen or so figures stood at a safe distance surrounding the burning plane, pointing at its trapped occupant. The brightness of the flames gave Carmichael the cover he needed. Using the shotgun, he pushed himself to his feet. He staggered towards the building he had seen, some kind of factory, he thought, with its big chimney. He looked back only once at the wreckage; poor Corbett's funeral pyre.

*

Lieutenant Smith cantered up towards Harry and the others. 'We're going to try to take the pressure off the Cheshires and Norfolks to our right,' he said, waving an arm in an easterly direction. Harry's eyes followed the outstretched hand, and he saw the two battalions. Beyond them, he noticed the British artillery holding the right of the line. All around them, German troops occupied the roads and fields, pushing hard.

'We're going to lead a charge at the guns up by that factory.'

The men looked north, and a mile or so distant, they could see the sugar factory, its chimney visible for miles and, just beyond, the German artillery that were causing such a misery for the British infantry.

'We'll capture the guns and send Jerry running.' Smith, grinning, turned to face north, and Harry nudged Lucy forwards so that he would be ready with his bugle at his officer's side.

Smith leaned round in his saddle. 'The 9th Lancers are coming with us, but I want us to be first into the action, Thatcher.'

Harry nodded, and felt the familiar nausea. He thought he might actually be sick, and he leaned out of his saddle. Just then, Smith drew his sword, and Lucy quivered at the sound of the metal blade scraping from its scabbard. The rest of the men of the two squadrons assigned to the charge drew their blades, and the horses were all up on their toes, knowing that sound presaged the charge; the thrill of the gallop.

Lucy stepped from side to side, keen to get going, and Harry pulled at her bit, holding her, the distraction from his fear welcome. Smith turned and nodded to him, and Harry, his mouth suddenly dry, licked his lips. He put the bugle to his mouth and blew the signal to advance.

Lucy's head went up, and Dancer skipped sideways. Smith tugged at the reins, holding him in check, holding him back until the moment when he would unleash him at the enemy gunners. The line advanced, slightly uneven as each horse sought to get ahead of those either side. The sword blades shone in the summer sun, and Harry couldn't help grinning over to Thomson. It was magnificent.

At a shout from Smith, Harry signalled the charge, and the horses needed no urging; they were desperate to run. Lucy's neck stretched long as her stride increased, the motion becoming suddenly smooth beneath Harry as she began to gallop. Dancer sensed her coming up on his right, and he was having none of it. He strained every muscle in his body to keep the mare behind him.

Smith lowered his blade, locked his elbow, and stared ahead at the German guns, coming rapidly closer now. The sugar factory was three hundred or so yards ahead, the gunners beyond. And then the gunners opened fire at the approaching threat.

In the sugar factory, Harry saw something flashing. With a cold dread, he realised it was the muzzle flashes of a machine-gun. The man to Harry's left let go of his reins and toppled backwards off his mount; the horse hardly checked, but instead, began to pull ahead unencumbered by the weight of his rider. Harry looked back over his shoulder, but he couldn't see the man; he'd disappeared into a forest of horses' hooves.

*

Carmichael had spent the morning nursing his wounds and hiding in a deserted office, crouching beneath a desk. Papers were scattered over the floor, and there was even a half drunk cup of coffee on the desk, as if the occupant of the office had been hurriedly called away, and had not returned.

The machine-gun began firing again, and Carmichael turned his head to try to place the sound; it seemed as if the they were above him, presumably giving them an excellent field of fire.

He opened Corbett's shotgun and removed each cartridge. Neither had been fired, and he inserted them back into the weapon, leaving the shotgun hinged open. The machine-gun was still firing, and although he didn't know at whom, he knew it must be friendly forces and he felt he had to do something about it. He pulled himself out from his hiding place and stood up, his shoulder knocking into the desk, spilling the remains of the coffee over the paperwork and accounts ledgers.

He looked over to the door, and hesitated a moment. Then he walked towards the door, the shotgun held in the crook of his elbow as if he were out on his estate, shooting grouse. He grinned at his own stupidity, and after closing the shotgun with a satisfying metallic clunk, he began climbing the stairs that led up into other offices above the factory floor.

*

Thomson shouted aloud, a meaningless cry that gave voice to his exultation, banishing his fear to the recesses of his mind. The distance was closing: a hundred yards, and then they would be past the factory and up to the enemy gunners. The horse and man ahead dissolved into a burst of red. A shell had exploded right on them, and they were literally blasted to fragments. Thomson rode through the cloud of blood without checking.

Off to their left, German infantry lying prone in shallow scrapes in the soil began to shoot at the charging enemy cavalry. It wasn't possible to aim, to pick out a single horseman; but there was no need. The charge was a solid block of horse and man, and any bullet must surely find a target.

The sugar factory was very close now, and the machine-gun would soon be unable to bear on them, and perhaps the worst would be past. Harry gripped his own sword tight, and made ready to clash with the gunners. He could see the artillery line, a few yards separating each of the field guns. They would slice between them, their blades cutting and thrusting, and the gunners would run from the charge. They would chase them down, their blades cutting back as they leaned out of their saddles to kill the enemy. They would capture the guns, and it would be glorious.

Harry had dropped back, Dancer's strength ensuring he was a few lengths ahead of Lucy, and suddenly the horse was down: a tumbling, twirling mess of legs and rider and Smith's sword arm. And then Harry saw why: a three-stranded, barbed wire fence, invisible until now. He readied himself to jump, but Lucy hadn't seen the obstacle. He pulled hard at the reins, knowing that he couldn't stop her, and she tried to respond, although she wanted to run on. And then the wire caught her chest and legs, and she fell heavily, the wire tearing into her flesh, cutting her legs to the bone and opening a long gash down her shoulder.

Harry found himself airborne, and he landed ten, maybe fifteen yards further on, the air crushed from his chest. He lay still for a moment, struggling to inflate his lungs, and then he turned his head to face back the way they'd come. The wire had created total chaos. The beauty of the charge had dissolved in seconds to a confused scrum as riders sought to avoid the wire, the enfilading rifle fire and each other.

The German infantry had no problem aiming their shots now. Here and there, a man would stand, shake himself down and thank his lucky stars, and then drop to enemy fire. Then the German gunners, who knew they had been safe behind the wire all along, opened fire, and the shrapnel flayed the survivors.

The charge stalled, and then in groups, men began to gallop back down the track, unable to progress further. In their wake, horses and men lay dead and wounded.

Harry looked across at Lucy. She was trying to stand, but the wire held her firm. She whinnied pitifully, and looked over to him, confused by the pain, wondering when he would come to help her. The German infantry was advancing, now, and it was obvious that the war was over for Harry, and anyone else still living.

*

The British field artillery guns fired from the east, and the enemy infantry returned to their scrapes. For the moment, Harry thought he was safe, so long as he could escape the attentions of the machine-gunners up in the factory. But it seemed that they'd lost interest in the tattered remnants of the cavalry charge, and were sending their lethal fire back down the track at the last of the retreating British horsemen.

Harry began to crawl slowly towards the wire. Lucy was lying on her side, having given up the struggle to get to her feet. Harry could see blood at her nose. She watched him as he approached. He managed to get up to her without incident, and then he stroked her muzzle. He looked down her body, and he realised that without cutters, he couldn't hope to get her out. Blood bubbled and frothed at her nose, and Harry knew that she had been struck in the lungs; knew that there was nothing he could do to save her.

'Thatcher.'

Harry turned at the voice. 'Thomson?'

'Yes. You alright?'

'Yes, I'm fine. Where are you?'

'To your left, behind my horse. He's dead.'

Harry turned and looked along the line of the wire and, a few yards away, he saw Thomson's face peering around the end of his horse's nose.

'We must get out of here, Harry, otherwise we're going to spend the war locked up.'

Harry thought the idea of being locked up and unable to fight anymore sounded very attractive. 'Yes,' he said at length.

'Did Smith make it?'

Harry looked over. Dancer was right next to Lucy, just a few feet away. He could see the flies were settling on Dancer's eyes. Next to the horse, he spotted Lieutenant Smith's outstretched arm, his beautiful sword still held tight in his right hand.

'I don't think so.'

Lucy whinnied once more, her eyes rolling in her head. She was clearly in pain, and Harry knew he must do something. He murmured a few words to her. And then he stared at Smith's hand. He edged towards Dancer, disturbing the flies. He squeezed between Dancer and Lucy. Smith lay on his back, his eyes open and staring up at the sky. There was blood at his ear and nose, and Harry guessed he'd cracked his skull in the fall.

Moving slowly, hoping that no one was watching the fallen horses by the wire, he reached out and unclipped Smith's holster. He withdrew the lieutenant's service revolver, and then he edged back.

The machine-gun stopped. Harry lay next to Lucy again, and she stared at him, and he could see his own face reflected in her eyeball. He pressed the muzzle of the Webley to a point between her eyes, just as the vet had once shown them, back when they were training. 'Goes straight through their tiny brain,' he had said. 'Kills them quick and painless.' He remembered how he hadn't really been listening. There was no thought of a war, then, and so why would he need to know how to shoot his horse? But now, he hoped he was going to do it right. For Lucy. He squeezed the trigger a little, taking up the pressure, and waited. When the machine-gun began to fire, he squeezed again, and Lucy twitched once, and then lay still.

'You alright, Harry?' said Thomson, surprised at the closeness of the shot.

Harry didn't answer, but Thomson could hear crying, and he realised what must have happened. He lay still, and waited until the crying stopped. He had to wait a long time.

*

Thomson crawled over towards Harry's hiding place between the two dead horses. It took him fully fifteen minutes because he daren't move more than a few inches at a time for fear of attracting the attentions of the machine-gun team in their eyrie up in the sugar factory. He stared at Smith's corpse for a few moments. 'Alright, Harry?'

'They're all dead, Thomson.'

'No they're not, Harry. Just a few. The others rode back. I saw them go.'

He reached out and put his hand onto Harry's shoulder. The lad jumped at the physical contact. 'Listen, Thatcher,' the surname this time, because this was all business. 'We need to get out of here.'

Harry stared back at Thomson, his eyes wide, red-rimmed.

'We can't just stay put. We'll either end up prisoners, or dead.' He didn't say more, decided to let his words sink in for a bit. He edged over towards Smith and pulled the man's water bottle free. He took a deep swig and then wiped his mouth before handing the canteen to Harry.

Harry took the water and without thinking, he drank until the canteen was empty.

'No, you go ahead, mate,' said Thomson. 'Finish it.' He grinned at Harry, and finally, Harry smiled back; a hesitant smile that barely touched his eyes, but a smile nonetheless.

'Right, Thatcher. Let's get going. The next time the gunner stops to load another belt, we're making for that factory and lose ourselves until nightfall. Then we'll see about getting back to the Regiment.'

'But the place is swarming with Germans, Thomson. We've no chance. It's better to stay put, I think.'

Thomson didn't argue. 'When he stops to reload, run like blazes for the wall over there.' He pointed at brick wall forty or fifty yards away that ran around the factory. 'When you get there, climb over and then stay still.'

Harry just looked at him. Thomson reached past the lad and pulled his rifle from the bucket on Lucy's tack. Then he unfastened the buckle of the bandolier that was around her neck. He wasn't sure he would be able to get it free from beneath her deadweight; he would find out when they stood up.

The gun stopped firing, and Thomson was on his feet. 'Go!'

Despite the almost overwhelming desire to stay lying between the horses, Harry stood and began to run towards the distant wall. Thomson gave the bandolier a tug, and it came free, the flies crawling in Lucy's head wound coming up in a great buzzing cloud. But Thomson was already on his way, a few yards behind Harry, his arms pumping, the bandolier slapping his leg with each long stride.

They were halfway when the gunners must have seen them, and only a few feet in front of Harry, the soil was being churned up as over four hundred rounds per minute tore into the ground around them. The wall was still thirty yards away, and it may as well have been thirty miles. They would never make it.

*

The gun opened up again, and Carmichael knew he couldn't wait. He threw himself into the room. Four men were crouched around their Spandau MG08 machine-gun. It sat on a tripod, the large water-cooled barrel protruding through a window that overlooked the battlefield. One of the men turned around at the sound of Carmichael's sudden arrival and began to come to his feet.

Carmichael fired, not worrying about aiming, knowing that the pellets in the cartridge would spread out, and by the time they reached the far side of the room, they would certainly hit the man. The first German fell back, his chest torn open, quite dead before he hit the wooden floor.

Two others stood, and the wind of a bullet's passing ruffled Carmichael's hair. The two enemy gunners were each armed with a Luger pistol, and before either man could get off another shot, Carmichael fired again. The pellets struck one of the men full in his face, leaving a red pulp in its place. His comrade lowered his weapon, but before he could surrender, Carmichael had dropped the shotgun.

The German realised the enemy officer's weapon was empty, and he smiled as he brought his Luger back up, stretching out his right arm. But Carmichael had his own sidearm in his hand, his arm coming up to the firing position. Crack. The German fired first, but the shot went wide; the bullet buried itself in a bookcase on the far side of the office. The Webley's roar filled the room as Carmichael squeezed the trigger. The bullet struck the enemy gunner in his chest, and he toppled forward. But Carmichael wasn't watching. He turned his attention to the last man of the team, the number one. The machine-gun was silent as the German reached for his own sidearm, turning to face this surprise attack. But he was too slow, and the fear showed in his face for a moment, to be replaced, thought Carmichael, by an expression of resignation. Carmichael's second round passed through the gunner's upper teeth and through his throat. He clawed at his neck as he fell back, the blood squirting between his fingers, thick and dark as his heart continued to pump hard and fast.

Carmichael walked over, looked down at the man. The German looked back up, but he didn't seem to see Carmichael, too lost in his futile fight for life. Carmichael, who had been raised a country boy and knew what to do with a wounded animal, fired again. The German's leg twitched twice, and then he was still.

*

Harry reached the wall first, but Thomson was a split-second behind him. He'd no idea why the gun had stopped firing, he just knew it had. He jumped and easily reached over the six foot wall. His boots scrabbled for a second, got purchase, and then he heaved himself up, and then rolled like a sausage over the top. He crashed to the ground, and groaned.

A rifle landed nearby, and then looking up, Harry saw Thomson coming over. 'Come on, Thatcher,' he said, bending to grab the Lee Enfield rifle as he ran by.

Harry got to his feet and the two raced for a pair of doors a short distance ahead that led into the factory buildings and, with luck, to safety.

Nine

Carmichael leaned out of the window, saw the two British cavalrymen running for the wall, and knew that his action had probably saved them. He turned away and stepped over the dead German without looking down at the horror the heavy bullet from the Webley had wrought. Holstering his sidearm, he walked across the room. When he reached the door, he bent to collect the shotgun, stood, and cracked it open. He removed the spent cartridges, releasing a thin wisp of smoke from each barrel. Out of the corner of his eye, he noticed that his boots had left bloody prints across the oak floorboards. He shivered with revulsion, and then left the room.

He walked as quietly as possible because, although he had not seen any other enemy troops, he didn't doubt there would be more coming now that the machine-gun had stopped firing. Arriving on the next floor, he stopped and listened. He knew that the cavalrymen he had seen would be somewhere in the factory, and it made sense to meet up with them; they would stand a better chance if they were together.

*

Harry leaned over, his hands on his knees. His stomach heaved again, but there was nothing left to bring up.

'It's the excitement, the thrill. Body finds it difficult to cope. Nothing to be ashamed of.' Thomson patted Harry on the back.

Harry wiped the ribbon of drool from his mouth. He was finding it all too much. Half an hour ago, he'd been sitting next to Lieutenant Smith looking at this factory from the safety of the rest of the Cavalry Division. And now, his horse was dead. Lieutenant Smith was dead. They were lost behind enemy lines and he had no idea how he was ever to get back. His stomach heaved again, and he gagged, leaning over.

Thomson turned at a noise behind them, instinctively bringing his rifle up.

'Steady, Trooper.' Carmichael lifted a placatory hand. 'I'm on your side.' He looked at Harry. 'Is he alright?'

Thomson saw a young officer, his uniform torn and dirty. He noticed the wings on his tunic and a shotgun tucked over his forearm. He couldn't help smiling. 'Yes, Sir. Just been a bit of a morning for us both. Was that you that stopped the machine-gun, Sir?'

'Thought I might be able to help.'

'Thanks,' said Thomson, and then after failing to come up with a word to express the depth of his gratitude, he added more quietly, 'Thanks.'

Carmichael smiled. 'Now, any thoughts as to how we might get out of here?'

Thomson shook his head. 'Luckily, you're the senior officer, Sir. Before we do escape, though, we could do with something to eat.' He glanced at Harry. 'Well, I could, anyway.'

'I didn't think to bring anything when Jerry shot down my plane.'

'You fly?' Harry looked up suddenly.

'Yes, lad, I fly.'

'What's that like? I mean,' and then, lost for words, 'what's it like?'

'It's like nothing you've ever done. Nothing.'

Thomson looked between the two of them. 'Well, I'm still hungry. We should try to find something to eat.'

Carmichael thought for a moment. 'The Germans upstairs, the machine-gun team. They'll have some food. They were probably expecting to be up there all day.'

'Right, let's get their supplies and then go and find somewhere quiet to rest up before their mates come and look for them.'

Carmichael led them back the stairs and into the room at the front of the factory where the German machine-gunners lay.

'Blimey,' said Thomson. 'You did this?' He looked at the carnage at his feet, one man with almost his whole head gone. Carmichael didn't respond, and decided he couldn't look.

'Right,' said Thomson, getting down to business. 'I'll check their packs for food and drink. Thatcher, you stand guard at the top of the stairs,' he said, seeing the look on Harry's face, before handing Harry the rifle. Harry walked to the door and stepped out onto the landing. He took up a position at the top of the stairs that enabled him to see down the stairwell.

'Lieutenant?' Carmichael turned. 'That machine-gun's loaded. Why don't you kneel behind it and fire off a belt into the middle of nowhere?' Carmichael looked at him blankly. 'Because,' said Thomson, answering the unasked question,

'Jerry will think their boys are alright and might not come to check up on them.' He looked across the room. 'Looks like they were expecting to be up here a while.' He indicated the boxes of machine-gun ammunition stacked against the far wall.

While Thomson turned each of the Germans over, going through their packs for food, Carmichael knelt in a sticky pool of congealing blood, and looking over the sights of the MG08, he pressed the firing button. His rounds struck the ground harmlessly a few hundred yards away. When the gun clicked on an empty chamber, he stood and stepped back from the window. He took a last look across at the British divisions on the low hills opposite, knew they'd be gone by nightfall, and wondered whether he was destined to spend the war in Germany.

'Come on,' said the trooper. 'We've got what we need.' Thomson was carrying four water bottles and two German packs stuffed with various provisions, including a loaf of bread that Carmichael could see poking out of the top of one of them.

Harry turned at their approach. 'All quiet,' he said. The three of them made their way downstairs, Carmichael leading them to the office on the ground floor he'd been hiding in earlier.

'We can't stay here, Sir,' said Thomson.

'Why not?'

'Because Jerry is bound to use the factory later. We'll be found for sure, wherever we hide. The place will be swarming with them.'

Carmichael looked at the cavalry trooper. 'Alright. Ideas?'

'I noticed a deep drain on our way into the factory. There's a tunnel we could hide in. There shouldn't be any water or anything coming down the drain because no one's been using the factory for a bit.'

'Right, lead on, then.'

They continued down the last flight of wooden steps onto the factory floor. To their left, the door through which Thomson and Harry had arrived earlier. 'Take these,' Thomson said, handing Harry the two German packs and the water bottles he'd liberated from their former owners. Harry took them, and Thomson crossed to the door. He leaned slowly out of the doorway. He could see enemy troops moving about some distance away, but he reckoned the height of the wall around the factory should shield them as they made their move.

He turned and nodded once, and then was gone, keeping low as he ran. Carmichael crossed to the doorway with Harry just behind him. He, too, stopped before stepping into the sunlight and leaned out as Thomson had done. A couple of dozen yards away was a runnel, brick lined with a metal grating as a cover. It continued towards the outer wall where it disappeared beneath the ground, presumably to a soakaway, or perhaps a stream or river course.

Thomson was kneeling at the edge of the runnel and had levered a piece of the grating up with a pocket knife. He pushed it to one side, and signalled to the others.

Carmichael and Harry ran across the dusty yard and stopped next to Thomson.

'In you go, Thatcher,' said Thomson.

Dropping the German packs at his feet, Harry stepped down into the drain. He picked up the packs, slung them over his shoulders and dropped to his hands and knees. He began to crawl towards the outer wall of the sugar factory, the drain edging deeper as he went. Although there was a musty smell to the place, as Thomson had guessed, it wasn't wet, and Harry didn't find the smell unpleasant. He passed beneath the point where the drain went underground and he continued for a few yards further on. He reckoned he was beneath the perimeter wall, now, and so he stopped. Looking further along, he could see daylight, and so somewhere, the drain opened up again.

'Alright, Trooper?'

It was the officer. Harry nodded. 'Yes, Sir.'

Harry looked back the way they'd come and watched while Thomson dropped into the drainage channel. He grunted as he dragged the grating back into place. It fell with a clank, and then Thomson was scuttling towards them. 'We should be safe enough here,' he said. 'Now, how about something to eat?'

The three of them sat, legs outstretched and backs against the cool wall, chewing on their liberated lunch. Now that the excitement had passed, the fear had become manageable, and Harry found that he was hungry. But he wasn't sure about the sausage that Thomson handed him and gave it a suspicious sniff.

'Best in the world. Germans are famous for them.'

Harry took a bite, and although it was a little too spicy, it was delicious.

'So, Lieutenant. What's the plan?' said Thomson, talking around a mouthful.

Carmichael swallowed and wiped his hand across his mouth. 'I suggest we lay low until dark, and then we try to get back to British lines. We're retreating, so …'

'Retreating? No,' said Thomson, 'we're repositioning, Sir.'

'Call it what you want, er …'

'Thomson, Sir.'

'Thomson. But the truth is, we're outnumbered almost three to one here, and there is no way we can outfight these Germans. All we can do is get out of their way. If we retreat, we shorten our line and can concentrate more troops in one place. And perhaps that will be enough. To hold them, at least.'

Thomson didn't respond immediately, but after a minute, said: 'But we gave them a bloody nose yesterday, Sir. At Mons.'

'You did, but it's not enough. There are just too many of them, Thomson. I can assure you that our army will retreat; a headlong retreat. And if we want to get home, we're going to have to try to keep up with them.'

Harry watched the two older men talking, and he felt his fear return. His stomach rebelled at the rich sausage and he stopped eating. Carmichael looked over towards him. 'What's your name, Trooper?'

'Thatcher, Sir.'

'I'm Lieutenant Carmichael. Well, Thatcher, we'll be alright, don't you worry.'

Thomson was still silent, staring into space. 'They said it would be over by Christmas,' he said to no one in particular. 'I actually thought that we might miss out on all the action;

that it would be finished before the Cavalry Division got here.'

Carmichael looked at him. 'Our job, Thomson – the job of the BEF – is to cover the left flank of the French Fifth Army. They are retreating. I've seen it myself; and we must go with them.' He took a drink from one of the German canteens and then continued: 'So, I doubt it will be over by next Christmas, Thomson, let alone this one. If we get back to our own lines, I assure you, you'll see plenty more action. Now, when I overflew the area earlier, I noticed a couple of villages hereabouts. Perhaps the best thing is to make our way to one of those, acquire more supplies, and then push on through the night.'

Thomson looked across to Harry, and then back to Carmichael. 'Right you are, Sir.'

From further along the ditch, there was a crash as boots landed on the metal grating. Harry and the other two looked around in surprise at the sudden sound. Voices, excited and urgent. Harry recognised some of what was being said. Although he hadn't studied German at school, they'd had a German maths teacher, and he had taken to teaching Harry a little of his language. Officers calling orders to their men, and Harry could hear the sound of soldiers running around the yard they'd just left.

There were shouts from further away now, and then the sound of a machine-gun. Harry guessed that they'd found their dead comrades, and even now were presumably searching the entire factory, room by room, for whoever had killed them.

Thomson lifted the rifle across his lap without making a sound, and gently, slowly, he eased the bolt back to check that it was loaded before sliding it forward once more. The metallic click of the action was horrifyingly loud in the confined space of the drainage tunnel.

Carmichael picked up Corbett's shotgun and levered it open. He reached into the canvas bag he still carried over his shoulder and inserted two fresh cartridges. In the close confines of the tunnel, it would be a fearsome weapon. He looked across to Harry, and then shifting his weight onto one buttock, he reached for his pistol and handed it across to Harry.

The Webley was heavier than Harry had expected. He'd seen the effects of the weapon upstairs in the office, and it gave him some confidence.

The three of them waited, straining to hear what was going on up above them. It was obvious that the Germans were moving into the factory, and the machine-gun continued firing.

The tunnel suddenly darkened as a score of men stood in a line across the gratings. Harry looked down at his hand, noticed that it had begun to shake, and he struggled to make it stop. By gripping the pistol hard, he managed to control the outward signs of his fear. A command was shouted, and then the line of soldiers marched off. The three shared a look, but no one dared speak.

*

'I'm going to have a look to see what's going on outside, Sir,' said Harry.

Carmichael nodded. 'Be careful.'

Harry crawled past Thomson and on down the drainage channel towards the distant light. As it grew closer, the sounds of the German artillery became louder, echoing off the brick walls of the drain. He reached the last few yards of the channel before it opened to the daylight and he could see enemy troops coming past. And then a German soldier came right to the ditch. One of his friends shouted something, and he shouted back. There was laughing, and then the soldier came straight to the opening of the tunnel and stood there, feet from Harry's hiding place; he shrank back, terrified that he would be seen. But from the outside, the drainage ditch was utterly dark. He waited, unsure what the man would do. And then the man began to urinate into the ditch, and there was more laughter from his friends. He fastened his breeches, and then was gone.

Harry let out a long, slow breath. He knew he couldn't risk sticking his head up in broad daylight to see what else was going on, and so there was no point going further. He turned in the tunnel and headed back the way he had come.

'Well?'

'The Germans are still advancing, Sir. Hundreds, probably thousands of them.'

'We can't possibly move until nightfall,' said Thomson.

'Agreed. We should try to get some sleep, then,' said Carmichael. Thomson nodded and turned so that his back rested against the brick. He closed his eyes, and Harry saw that within a few minutes, his breathing had become regular and slow. He was asleep! He turned to say something to the Lieutenant, but he, too, appeared to be asleep.

Harry closed his eyes, but images of the cavalry charge, of the man blown to tatters beside him, of the flies on Smith's face, kept his mind racing. He thought of his horse, of the hideous wounds on the Germans upstairs in the factory offices, of his brother Richard out there in the artillery duel with the Germans and, despite all this, sleep came.

Ten

It was pitch dark when Harry woke. He couldn't see the others at first, and he panicked, unsure of where he was. He looked left and right, could just make out a lighter patch either side, and then he remembered that they were lying in the drainage ditch at the sugar factory.

There was a noise and, as Harry turned, the distant light to his left was blocked out. His heart began to pump hard and fast in his chest, and he made to turn and run, but a quiet voice stopped him: 'I think it's alright.' It was Thomson. 'They're still around here, but we've got a chance in the darkness. We can't go back into the yard, obviously, so we'll go the other way.'

'I think we should head for Élouges,' said Carmichael. 'It's the right direction, and what's more, it should be easy to find. The railway lines run past the factory straight to the village. Come on.'

'You awake, Thatcher?' said Thomson.

'Yes.'

'Come on, then. Bring the rest of the food, will you?'

After stuffing the remains of their food into one of the packs, Harry pushed the Webley on top and then slipped his arms through the pack's straps. He began to crawl after the others towards the open end of the drainage channel. He found the other two crouched low in some undergrowth that had sprouted in the rich moist soil around the end of the ditch. Although it was the middle of the night, Harry could make out the rail tracks shining some distance away. No one spoke, but Thomson stood and began to walk past the factory.

The three walked in a line, some few yards separating each of them, with Carmichael bringing up the rear of their little group. They passed close to the outer wall of the factory, and Harry heard German voices.

Thomson decided the factory was a little close for comfort, and he angled away towards the tracks. He climbed up the shingle bed and stepped over, walking towards a small copse of trees beyond.

'Wer ist da?'

The voice stopped Carmichael cold. He turned around, and a few yards away, a German infantryman stood. The man repeated his question, his voice unconcerned. He didn't really expect there to be any enemy soldiers wandering around, but he had his orders, and so he would stop anyone he saw.

Carmichael opened his mouth to speak, wondering if his French might do the trick; perhaps he could pass as a local?

'Was machen Sie?' said the German, more demanding this time.

And then, from behind Carmichael: *'Wir haben den Wald für englische Soldaten zu suchen,'* said Harry.

The sentry hesitated. He knew of no such orders but, like all Germans, he had a healthy respect for authority. And he could see that the young speaker had on a German pack. He shrugged. *'Gute Jagd,'* he said, losing interest, wanting to be back with his friends, smoking by the factory wall.

'*Danke.*' Harry took Carmichael by the arm and hurried him across towards the tracks.

'What did you tell him, Thatcher?' said Carmichael when they were safely out of earshot.

'I told him we had orders to search for English soldiers in the woods, Sir.'

'Good thinking. Well done, lad.'

'He wished us good hunting.'

Carmichael laughed. 'Did he? Well done indeed, Thatcher.'

'My father always thought that book learning was a waste of time, Sir.'

'Indeed? Well, you'll be able to set him straight when we get back to England.'

'Alright you two?'

'We're fine, Thomson. Had a run in with a German sentry, but Thatcher here dealt with it.'

Thomson looked at Harry's shadowy figure, but couldn't make out his face. 'Come on, then. We must get to the village and on our way before dawn.'

*

As they approached Élouges, it became obvious that it wouldn't be easy to find any food or drink from the locals; the streets were crowded with German soldiers. They were still on the march, still chasing after the departing BEF, but an army of almost two hundred thousand men leaves a long wake behind it.

'What are we going to do?' said Thomson.

The three of them were kneeling behind low bushes at the edge of a small wood a mile or so from the village. Carmichael rubbed his chin, feeling the stubble beneath his fingertips. He looked to the east, to their left. About a half a mile away, he spotted a collection of farm buildings. 'There,' he said. 'Come on.'

They walked cautiously towards the farm. Glancing behind them, Thomson saw the lines of German infantry using the railway lines as a convenient marker for moving across the darkened fields and yards. None seemed to be heading their way.

Carmichael stopped at the margin of the farm, crouching behind a low wall. He raised his head and looked over the wall into the midden beyond. 'It looks alright, but there could be Germans billeted in the outbuildings.'

A dog began to bark, and Carmichael, halfway to his feet, froze. After a second, he dropped back down, but the dog carried on barking; whether this was because of their presence, he couldn't know. Across the yard, a door opened. A man was silhouetted against a dim light coming from the room behind him. He shouted, his words a thickly accented French.

The dog stopped its incessant noise, and the man closed the door.

'I'll go, Sir,' said Harry.

'Wait.' Thomson grabbed his arm.

'It makes sense, Thomson. I can speak French. And in any case, if there's Germans there, I'm no great loss to the war effort, am I?' Harry pulled free of Thomson's grip and crossed the yard. Summoning his courage, he forced himself not look back at his comrades. The dog, lying chained a few yards from the door of the farm, looked up at him with interest, but didn't bark. Harry knelt and ruffled the dog's ears. It seemed pleased to see him, licking at his hand. Standing straight, he rapped on the door.

He could hear the man, presumably the farmer, cursing from within. The farmer yanked open the door, ready to shout obscenities at whoever he found waiting, but he saw only a young lad in a uniform perhaps a size too big for him; and not a Belgian uniform, nor French. He turned and retrieved a lamp from a table behind him and, holding it up, he studied Harry before deciding he was harmless.

The others watched Harry from across the yard. After a moment, Harry pointed in their direction. The man considered, and then he gestured Harry inside. Harry turned and waved them over. Carmichael opened the shotgun to make it safe, Thomson shouldered his rifle, and the two walked towards the open kitchen door.

Inside, an old woman moved around the stove, preparing something for them to eat. Harry turned as the others came in. 'She's making us soup.'

'What did the old man say?' Thomson nodded towards the farmer who sat at the head of his table, still in his night things.

'We can eat something here and then sleep in the barn, but he wants us gone before dawn.'

'We shan't be staying,' said Carmichael, putting the shotgun down on the table. 'It's too dangerous. For us and for them.'

The farmer's wife took the saucepan from the stovetop and turning, frowned at Carmichael's shotgun. He moved it, placing it on the floor within easy reach. She took three wooden bowls down from the simple dresser behind her husband and set them on the table.

The old man spoke, and she nodded, going to the larder. She returned with a bottle of wine and a half loaf of bread. The bottle had no markings, and so Harry assumed it was homemade. She ladled a generous helping of thick soup into each bowl.

'*Merci beaucoup*,' said Carmichael, picking up the first bowl and taking a spoon.

The old man nodded, and then indicated the chairs with a wave of his hand. Carmichael sat at the far end of the table, and Thomson and Harry either side. The old woman stood by her husband as he cut thick slices off the loaf.

Harry remembered his manners and took off his cap, placing it on the dresser behind him. The old woman smiled at him, and then frowned at Thomson who had begun eating, his own cap still firmly on his head. He was too hungry to notice.

Chicken, thought Harry as he swallowed a mouthful, and it was probably the best thing he'd had to eat in a long time. He wasn't much of a drinker, but the strong, rough wine was welcome, taking the edge of the day's trials.

'We must go,' said Carmichael at last, wiping his mouth with a handkerchief he produced from his trousers pocket. 'Tell them we're going to leave, and thank them, Thatcher.'

Harry nodded, and made the translation. The old woman went to the larder and came back with a big piece of hard cheese and another loaf of bread. Her husband said something, a fierce frown on his face, but she ignored him and folded the cheese into a muslin before she handed it and the bread to Harry. He thanked her, and pushed them into the German pack at his feet alongside the remains of the German sausage. Harry held up his water bottles, and the farmer muttered something, pointing to the door.

'In the yard, Sir,' said Harry, 'there's a pump. We can fill them there.'

Thomson finished chasing the last of his soup around the bowl and stood. He went to the old woman. 'That was the best soup I've had in an age.' He kissed her on her cheek. She grinned, blushed, and began to clear away the bowls.

The dog started to bark again, and the farmer made to shout at him, but Carmichael held up a hand. 'Have a look, Thomson.' The five of them stared at the door, and then Thomson walked to the shuttered window that overlooked the yard. He opened the shutters the smallest crack, and through the gap he could make out the unmistakeable shape of men armed with rifles slung over their shoulders. They were coming into the yard; probably not suspicious, just hungry.

'Jerry,' he said, turning from the window.

Harry fired off some French and the colour drained from the old woman's face. The farmer stood, and began talking hurriedly to Harry. He nodded, and then turned to Carmichael. 'This way, Sir,' he said, and grabbing his pack, he led them to the far side of the small kitchen. Pushing open the door, the three of them went through into the small parlour beyond. A window opened onto the rear of the farmhouse, and Harry clambered through, pushing the pack before him.

No sooner had they got clear of the back of the house than German voices could be heard from within. 'They'll be fine,' said Carmichael. 'They're civilians. They're not involved.'

Thomson and Carmichael followed Harry as he led them around the back of a barn that joined the farmhouse at a right-angle. The three squeezed through the barn door, and Harry crossed to the other side where he could see the front of the farmhouse.

The dog was still barking, but a German soldier was kneeling beside it, making as if to stroke the animal. Dogs were dogs and men were men, thought Harry, smiling. He turned, ready to leave, but a sudden shout made him spin round.

The farmer was being pushed out of his kitchen, and the man stroking the dog stood back, and unslung his rifle, bringing it up to his shoulder and turning around to scan the yard behind him. Harry instinctively moved into the shadows.

'What's going on?'

'Not sure, Sir.'

Another soldier came out, dragging the old woman and threw her against the farmer. The farmer put his arm around his wife, and the two stood in the puddle of light thrown by the kitchen lamps. A soldier, an officer by the looks of the uniform, thought Harry, came out, and with horror, Harry recognised what he held in his hand: his own service cap.

The German officer began screaming into the faces of the farmer and his wife, waving the cap at them, but neither said anything.

'We must do something, Sir.'

Thomson crowded next to Harry, staring across at the unfolding scene. The dog was going berserk, straining at the chain that held him to the farmhouse wall. The officer lost his patience, withdrew his sidearm, and without hesitation, shot the dog. The soldier who had earlier petted the animal looked aghast, but said nothing.

Thomson unslung his rifle, making ready to crash through the doors and deal with the officer, but Carmichael's hand was at his shoulder. 'It's just a dog, Thomson. No point getting yourself killed over a dog.'

The woman cried and made to move towards the dog, but her husband held her. The officer did not put away his pistol, and Harry knew something terrible would happen. The German officer shouted again, waving Harry's cap about. The old man gabbled something, but clearly it wasn't what the officer wanted to hear because he said something to his men. The three German soldiers stepped back, each man bringing up his rifle to point it at the two Belgians. The old couple looked at the Germans surrounding them, and Harry could hear the old woman's sniffles from across the yard. And then the officer lifted his pistol, pressing it to the woman's forehead. He spoke to the old man, too quietly for Harry to hear the words.

'No.' Thomson brought his rifle up so that the tip of the barrel protruded between the barn doors.

The pistol shot when it came was surprisingly loud, and the old woman dropped to the ground. The farmer cried out, a cry full of anguish. Thomson fired, and the bullet from his Lee Enfield struck the officer in his chest, bursting his heart as it passed through his body and on into the kitchen wall beyond. He dropped instantly, his Luger pistol falling from his dead hand, discharging a bullet as it struck the ground.

The three remaining soldiers turned at the sound of Thomson's rifle, but Thomson already had the next round in the chamber and without moving the weapon from the side of his head, he sent another bullet across the yard. It struck the soldier nearest the dog in his eye, a fluke in the dim light. But the other two had seen the rifle barrel, and began to fire back, two rounds clipping the doorframe near Harry's head.

Harry ducked back inside the barn just as Carmichael stepped out of it and walked across the muddy cobbles. His shotgun was closed, and he fired both barrels, one after the other. The two remaining Germans went down, and then Thomson ran over. He knelt at the farmer's side and looked down at the old man's wife, her shattered head cradled in his lap. Blood, dark and thick, puddled between his knees.

He shook his head and looked up at Carmichael. 'She's dead, Sir.' He stood and went to each of the Germans in turn. 'They're all done for, Sir.'

'We have to go. Come on.'

Harry pointed to the farmer. 'What about him?'

'We can't help him. We must go.'

Carmichael reloaded the shotgun and crossed the yard to the barn. Thomson checked the German corpses for anything they could use, and then he, too, turned and followed Carmichael.

Harry stood over the farmer and his wife. The man rocked back and forth on his knees, the world around him irrelevant now. Harry saw his service cap lying on the cobbles, gripped tightly in the dead German officer's left hand. Stepping over, he bent to retrieve it, but his hand came away, sticky with blood. With one more look at the distraught farmer, Harry turned around and walked away after the others.

Eleven

Harry couldn't get the image of the German officer out of his mind. Try as he might, it just played over and over: the pistol jumping in the officer's hand; the spent cartridge case spinning into the darkness; the woman stiffening, and then going slack and falling; the blood, a dark ribbon squirting from the hole in her forehead; the cry of her husband; the crack of Thomson's rifle. Again and again.

Thomson walked a little faster to catch Harry up. 'You alright, Thatcher?'

'I'm fine. I just keep thinking about the farmer. If I hadn't left my cap ...'

'There's little point in worrying about ifs, Thatcher,' said Carmichael, turning to speak over his shoulder. 'There was no need for that brutality, but this is war, and worse things will happen before it's done.'

'Yes, but if I'd only kept my cap on; but my mother says I should remove my hat indoors.'

'Your mother is quite right.'

Thomson put his hand on Harry's shoulder. 'You did nothing wrong, lad. Chances are, Jerry was just looking for trouble. For an excuse.'

The three had been walking for several hours. They'd no idea how far they'd travelled, they just kept walking south.

Carmichael was finding the shotgun heavy, and no matter where he rested it, within fifteen minutes, he was sore. Finally, he had taken to cradling the weapon across his two folded arms, and although this made walking a little awkward, he found the weight more bearable.

'I think we should stop for something to eat,' said Thomson.

'No. We must walk until it's light, and then hole up somewhere. We can't travel easily by day until we get past the German advance guard.'

Thomson didn't answer, but he knew the lieutenant was right. So he put his right foot in front of his left, and then his left foot in front of his right, and in that way, the hours of the night passed.

After the incident at the farm, they'd headed east towards a wood, running as fast as they could across the intervening open ground. Then they had turned due south, following a rough road that ran that direction, but keeping to the margins at the road's edge to avoid discovery. It was obvious an army had been that way: the ground was torn up by the passing of twenty thousand feet, but whether this was the fleeing British Expeditionary Force, or the pursuing Germans, they could not tell.

Harry lifted his head and, for the first time since they'd begun their march, he could see the back of Lieutenant Carmichael clearly; it was getting light.

'We ought to stop,' said Carmichael, as if sensing Harry's own thoughts. 'It'll be dawn soon.'

'I've been thinking, Sir,' said Harry. 'When we came up to Mons a few days back, we passed through a huge forest.

Took the Regiment a half day to ride through. We must be almost up to that now, Sir.'

Carmichael thought about it. Yes, he remembered the forest. It marked the border with France. He strained his eyes into the grey, pre-dawn light ahead. He felt certain that he could see a smudge of deeper darkness at the horizon. 'I think that could be the edge of the forest up yonder. Let's try for it before the sun comes up.' With that, he began to walk a little faster.

Harry decided that if they'd been horses, they'd have been trotting. His heavy German pack, his constant companion through the darkest hours of the night, now asserted its presence more strongly as it banged up and down on the raw skin of his shoulders. He bit his lip, ignored it, and tried to think of the rest they would have when they got to the forest.

*

'Ours or theirs?' Thomson looked back across the field they had just left. On the horizon, illuminated by the sun as it crept over the eastern treeline, he saw a line of advancing troops. The distant soldiers were walking through the same field of corn stooks that they had just left.

Carmichael turned. 'Germans,' he said, quite certain, used to identifying troops from a distance. 'Funny pointed helmets. Let's get moving into the trees.'

They carried on for a half hour until they felt safe, and then found a large fallen tree some distance off the track. They sat beneath the disc of its roots, torn from the soil by some long-forgotten storm.

Harry opened the pack and distributed the food. 'What kind of dog was it?' he said, biting off a piece of the remains of his part of the sausage.

Thomson, sitting a few feet away, shrugged and tore a bit off the loaf the old lady had given them.

'No idea,' said Carmichael, thinking suddenly of his own dogs. They'd be lying around the old range in the kitchen at home right now, waiting for the cook to come and start making the breakfast for the household. 'Friendly little chap, though.' He paused to swallow. 'I think we can risk carrying on through the forest during the day. We should be able to avoid detection. I would imagine that the enemy might pass to one side or the other.'

'Why, Sir?'

'It's no easy task threading an army of two hundred thousand men through woodland as thick as this. It would slow them down.'

Thomson nodded. 'I bet that's what our lads have done.'

'No doubt. The forest might be the most direct route south, but it's far too slow. In fact, we'll have to move quickly to catch them,' Carmichael said around a mouthful of bread. His mouth was dry, and it took him a moment to get the bread down his throat. He wished they'd remembered to bring water from the farm, but things had been a little hectic after the German officer had shot the old woman.

'We can rest for a bit, though, can't we?' Harry dreaded having to carry the pack so soon after taking it off.

Carmichael said nothing. He thought about the BEF passing to the west of the forest, heading, he supposed, for Paris. If they turned southwest, they could cut the corner and catch up. But what if the BEF had passed to the east, closer to where he supposed the French army to be? He chewed on another piece of bread as he thought about it.

'I don't think we can,' he said at last. 'Rest, that is. We have to keep going. I don't want to spend the war stuck in a prison camp somewhere, so we must keep going.'

Thomson wiped his greasy fingers on his trousers and reached out for his rifle. Ideally, he would have liked to have given it a clean, something he did every day without fail. He thought about doing so while the others finished their breakfasts, and began to take the small oil bottle and pull through from the aperture in the brass butt plate of the rifle.

Carmichael shook his head. 'No time, Thomson. We should get a move on.' The lieutenant made to get up, breadcrumbs dropping from his tunic onto the ground around him.

Thomson put away the cleaning kit and took a charger of five rounds of ammunition from his leather bandolier. He pulled back the rifle bolt, inserted the charger into the grooves of the rifle, and pushed the five rounds home into the magazine. Then he pushed the rifle bolt forwards and down, feeding a round into the breech.

Harry stood up, his legs shaking with the effort. He picked up the German pack. Carmichael handed him the remains of his breakfast: a small piece of sausage and another of cheese.

'I've got nothing left.' Thomson looked with envy at Carmichael's rations as Harry stowed them in the pack before hefting it over his shoulder. He pushed his left arm through the strap and was just attempting to slip his right arm through when a sudden noise stopped him. Someone was crashing through the undergrowth towards them; several someones, by the sounds of it.

Thomson turned fast to face the approaching sound, bringing his rifle to his shoulder. Carmichael, slower to react, grabbed at the shotgun that he had left leaning against the tree roots.

But he was too late.

*

Thomson's finger tightened on the trigger of his rifle as he waited for the enemy soldiers to come at them from around the back of the fallen tree trunk. There came a curious snuffling sound, and then trampling of at least a half dozen pairs of feet. Something appeared around the corner of the tree's root, and Thomson squeezed the trigger.

'No.' Harry's arm knocked at the rifle, and the bullet flew wide of its target. Thomson opened his mouth to protest, and then he saw what had caused Harry to cry out. The muzzle of a large, black horse. The horse whinnied and then blew loudly out of its nostrils. Thomson laughed, the tension gone.

'Here, boy.' Harry put out his hand as he walked up to the horse's head. He patted the animal's thick neck, and then he peered around the root disc. 'There's two more.'

'Well, that's a stroke of luck. Save us from walking all the way through the woods.' Thomson grinned at the lieutenant, but Carmichael didn't look overly happy at the news.

Thomson shouldered his rifle and followed Harry around the tree. Sure enough, two others horses stood just beyond the first: a grey and a bay. Harry walked to the other two horses and, as he took their reins in his hands, he talked to them, meaningless words in a soothing voice.

'How did they get here?' Carmichael stared across at the two horses Harry was leading back towards him. Harry stood to one side, and Carmichael could see a black smear across the hindquarters: blood, presumably from the horse's previous owner.

Thomson inspected the first horse, the black one. He checked its legs, running his hands up and down each one in turn, quickly assessing whether the animal had been injured. Harry did the same for the other two. 'They seem sound,' said Thomson. 'This should make for a quicker journey, Lieutenant.'

'You alright, Sir?' said Harry.

'Yes. It's just that, well, I've never ridden a horse.'

'Really, Sir? I thought all you gentlemen rode to hounds.' Thomson grinned at Harry.

'Not me, I'm afraid. I never took to the wretched creatures. Minds of their own, you know. I had a few lessons as a boy, but spent most of my time on my back in the exercise yard.'

'Well, Sir,' said Harry, looking up from checking each horse's tack, 'you've got a good opportunity to learn today. I'll take the grey; she reminds me a bit of Lucy. I think you'll be best on the big black one, Thomson.'

'Yes, I agree. He's more my size.'

'Yes, but he's also the curious one. He came to see what we were first, and I don't know that Lieutenant Carmichael would like a bold horse today. He'd be better with the bay mare, I reckon.'

The two looked at the brown horse, and it was quietly cropping at the grass, unconcerned about the goings on, possibly just happy to be back amongst men.

'Right.' Thomson slipped the bandolier he had been carrying since the cavalry charge over the black gelding's neck. He walked around the far side and seeing a Lee Enfield rifle already in the bucket, he looked over to Harry. 'You need a rifle, lad?'

Harry checked his new horse. 'Yes.' Thomson tossed his rifle towards Harry who caught it and slipped it into the leather sheath on the right side of the horse. 'The sword's still in the scabbard on this one,' said Harry. He checked the right side of Carmichael's bay for a rifle. No luck. 'You want my rifle, Sir?'

Carmichael shook his head. 'I think I'll stick with this,' he said, holding up the shotgun.

Harry stuck his boot toe into the left stirrup and heaved himself up into the saddle. It felt wonderful to be on a horse again. The grey lifted her head and turned to look at him out of the corner of her eye. He leaned forward and gave her neck a pat.

Thomson was already on his horse and was examining the newly acquired rifle. It was fully loaded. Satisfied, he slotted it back into the bucket behind his right leg. 'You alright, Sir?' he said, looking over to Carmichael.

Carmichael had watched the others mounting, and thought he would simply copy them. He nodded over to Thomson and then, to buy some time, he slipped his shotgun into the empty bucket on the horse's saddle. Then he began to walk around the animal, checking straps for tightness, patting the flanks and legs here and there, much as he checked his aircraft before each flight. He arrived back on the horse's left side with nothing further to delay him, and he lifted his right leg a little uncertainly. He realised his mistake, and before he climbed onto the horse to face backwards, he lowered his right leg and lifted his left. He glanced towards the others to see if they'd noticed. It didn't seem so.

When Carmichael looked away, Harry winked at Thomson who was grinning widely.

Carmichael pushed his left boot into the stirrup and just as he made to lift himself up, the horse took a small step. Carmichael hadn't expected the movement, and he stumbled, and unable to remove his boot, he fell backwards, his leg still stuck in the stirrup.

Thomson and Harry shared another look and tried hard not to laugh. 'It's not so easy the first time, Sir,' said Thomson, still grinning. Carmichael managed to get his foot free and rolled onto his knees and then stood up. He looked across at the other two and then began brushing the damp forest soil from the seat of his trousers. Thomson's smile had gone, his face a mask of seriousness.

'No,' said Carmichael. 'It's not, especially if the blessed animal's going to take off like that.' He turned and grasped the saddle's pommel in his left hand, and inserted his boot into the stirrup once more. He then began hopping at the side of the horse in his efforts to mount. The horse lifted its head from the thin grass of the forest floor and looked across at her two companions. Harry's grey whinnied, and the bay put back its head, bared its teeth in a bizarre smile, and neighed loudly before moving off towards another, richer patch of grass. Carmichael, with no wish to humiliate himself further, hopped alongside the plodding mare.

Thomson glanced at Harry, and then he nodded. 'Go on, Thatcher, give the Lieutenant a hand.'

Harry swung his right leg over his horse's head, and slipped off her left side. He handed his reins to Thomson to hold and then walked the few yards towards the red-faced Carmichael.

'Do you want me to hold her, Sir?' he said, and then, to ease Carmichael's embarrassment: 'Seems like you've got the lively one after all, Sir.'

'She does seem keen, doesn't she, Thatcher? And yes, perhaps you could hold her?'

Without saying anything, Harry walked to the bay's left side and linked his hands. 'Put your knee on my hands, Sir, and I'll give you a boost.'

Carmichael lifted his knee and placed it in the cradle of Harry' hands. Then as Harry lifted, he straightened his leg and found himself at saddle height. He flung his right leg over the horse's back, and then clung to the pommel with all his strength.

'Do you remember anything from your lessons, Sir?'

'I remember I prefer cars,' said Carmichael with a forced grin. The mare stretched her neck to try to reach an interesting branch, and Carmichael gasped aloud.

Harry turned to look over to Thomson. He sighed. 'Well, Sir,' said Harry. 'Take the reins.' He handed them to Carmichael. 'Hold them firm, but not tight, about here,' and he showed Carmichael where to grip them. 'When you want her to go right, you give some pressure on the right side, and she goes right. When you want her to go left, you pull back firmly, but not hard, with the left hand. Simple.'

Carmichael experimented, easing back on the reins first on one side, and then the other. The mare turned her head and looked at him over her right shoulder.

'You can also use the pressure of your legs, Sir. But first, we should get your feet into the stirrups.' Carmichael's legs hung straight down the sides of the horse as if he were sitting on a fence. 'They're a bit short for you, Sir. Hang on. Can you shift your leg forward, Sir?'

Carmichael moved his left leg forward, and Harry lifted the saddle up and loosened the stirrup strap, lengthening it. 'Can you slip your foot in, Sir?'

Carmichael looked down and tried to push the toe of his boot into the moving metal of the stirrup. A dimly remembered passage from the bible came to Harry's mind: something about threading a camel through the eye of a needle. 'Here, Sir,' he said at last, and grabbed Carmichael's boot and pushed it into the stirrup. He walked around the front of the mare and then repeated the process on the right side.

Finally, he walked to the front of the mare and held her by the bridle. 'Now, Sir, when you want her to go faster, you squeeze her with your calves. She knows that means go quick. When you want her to slow down, release the pressure and apply backwards force on both reins.'

Carmichael nodded. He felt like he had the first time he'd gone solo in the Avro, but then the fear had been tempered with excitement. Here, he was just frightened. He nodded again.

Harry saw Carmichael's knuckles were white where he gripped the reins with all his strength. 'You should probably ride between Thomson and me, Sir. I'll lead, and Thomson can bring up the rear.' He led the mare, turning her so she faced the same way as the other horses.

'There was that track we came in by,' said Thomson. 'We could pick that up not far through these trees and ride along it. Seem to remember it was heading south.'

'I've been thinking about that,' said Carmichael. 'I think we should head southwest. I imagine that the army has gone around the forest, and we can cut the corner and catch them up before they get to the other side.'

'But what if they've gone around the eastern edge, Sir?' Thomson gave voice to Carmichael's concern that they may, indeed, have tried to join with the French off to the southeast.

'Let's hope they have not, Thomson. We cannot second guess their decision, so we must gamble. If it were me, I would want to hold the Germans off the left flank, and that's best done by passing to the west. We just have to hope I'm right.'

'Well, let's start by heading down that track, and then look for a turn to the right. These hunting tracks criss-cross the forest, so it should be easy enough. Lead on, Harry.'

Harry, back in the saddle, turned and smiled at Carmichael. Then he squeezed his calves, and his horse responded immediately, and began to walk between the trees. Harry relaxed his grip on the reins and let his horse pick a good path. Every so often, he nudged her with a bit of leg pressure, directing her towards the track they had used when they came into the forest.

He turned back to look at Carmichael after a few yards, wanting to make sure he was still following, but also that he was still on the mare's back. Thomson waved from behind Carmichael, and so Harry turned to face front again, and the three began to make slow but steady progress through the trees.

Twelve

'Heels down, Sir.' Thomson had been giving the lieutenant the benefit of his equine knowledge since they had set off down the track. At first, Carmichael had thanked him, but now he merely grunted. Thomson smiled. He well remembered his first few hours in the saddle. Sore knees, sore arse and, thanks to a loose girth strap and a voluble corporal, a sore head.

Carmichael looked up at the sun, directly above. He knew that they must start to go west. He also knew they should go faster. He wiped the sweat from his brow. He hadn't realised quite how tiring simply sitting on a horse would be. He turned his head. 'We must go more quickly, and we must begin to bear southwest.'

'We can try trotting, Sir?'

'Then let's trot.'

'The movement is a little awkward, Sir. It's best to keep your backside firmly in the saddle; rising trot will be too tiring over the distance we have to ride.' Harry slowed and allowed Carmichael's horse to pull level with his own. 'When I set off, your horse will want to follow.' He looked at Carmichael, recognised the fear in his eyes. 'Come on, then, Sir.'

Harry clicked his tongue, and then urged his grey to a walk. He looked back at the others and, when they were all walking as before, he nudged his horse with his heels, and she began to trot on.

Carmichael's bay mare was keen to keep up with her friend, and she broke into a trot behind. Carmichael found the movement uncomfortable, the gait of the horse bumping him up and down in his saddle.

Harry looked back at the lieutenant and smiled. Carmichael's hands were coming up, the reins slack. It was a classic beginner mistake: the rider so busy trying to match the rhythm of the trot to ease the discomfort that they forgot everything else. When Carmichael's hands were in front of his face, as if he were conducting an orchestra, Harry called back. 'Drop your hands, Sir.'

Carmichael looked up, realised his arms were almost above his head for some reason, and dropped them back to the saddle.

'That's it, Sir,' said Harry, shouting back encouragement.

'Heels down, Sir,' came Thomson's voice from behind.

Carmichael cursed Thomson, cursed Harry and then he cursed his horse for good measure. He began to feel that he was being bumped out of his saddle, and he gripped with his legs, afraid of falling off. The mare interpreted the tightening grip of her rider's legs as an instruction to increase tempo, and she obediently broke into a canter. She saw a gap between the grey mare and the treeline at the edge of the track and she changed course slightly to squeeze through it.

'Slow down, Sir. I don't think we should risk a canter yet,' said Thomson. Harry turned at the shouted advice, and there was Carmichael, right behind him, his teeth bared in either terror or concentration; or perhaps both.

Carmichael couldn't remember how to slow a horse. He couldn't remember anything except that his legs would keep him in the saddle. The movement was easier now, the horse's strides longer, the motion smoother beneath him. As he passed Harry, the young trooper reached out to try to grab his reins, but the bay mare was enjoying herself: cavalry horses are bred for the charge. She looked across to Harry's grey mare. The grey's eyes rolled in her head and she tried to stretch her neck, pulling at the reins in Harry's hands.

Carmichael knew he would fall off, knew he would break his neck. He squeezed his legs tight around the horse's body and crouched as low in the saddle as he could. The pressure told his horse that more speed was wanted, and she was delighted to provide it. She began to gallop, covering the distance down the track at a blur.

Harry, open-mouthed with surprise, slackened the pressure on his reins and let his horse have her head. She took off after the bay, with Thomson some way behind.

The three men and their horses tore down the narrow hunting track, no more than four yards across. Carmichael was whipped by a low branch, and he cried out. Harry mistook the shout for excitement and he, too, whooped with the joy of it. The forest seemed to lean in, appearing as a dark green flash passing through their peripheral vision as they charged along.

Up ahead, Harry spotted a junction; a spur to the right at a forty five degree angle was about three hundred yards away. He wondered whether Carmichael had seen it. He urged the grey mare on, closing the gap with the lieutenant. The thump of the bay mare's hooves was louder as he drew closer, and clods of mud were thrown towards Harry, striking him and his horse.

The head of the grey drew level with the tail of Carmichael's bay mare. Harry dug in his heels and edged forward. Carmichael looked to his right as he caught sight of the grey's nose and, at that moment, Harry reached out of his saddle, stretching his left arm out to try to take the reins from Carmichael. 'Loosen your grip with your legs, Sir, and pull back hard on the reins.'

Carmichael stared across at Harry. Loosen his grip? Was the boy mad? His legs were the only things keeping him attached to the animal moving beneath him.

Harry looked up, and the junction was only yards away. He lunged at the reins, missed, and then he yanked at his right rein and sheared off, taking the right fork. Carmichael continued in a flat out gallop straight on.

'Damn.' Harry pulled his horse up in two body lengths before yanking her around and turning back. He put his heels to the mare, and they took off. Thomson flashed past him, following Carmichael, as Harry rounded the corner going in the other direction.

The bay mare, having lost its racing companion, began to slow and dropped out of the gallop quite suddenly. Carmichael, surprised by the rapid deceleration, was thrown forward against the animal's neck. His left foot slipped from the stirrup, and he lolled to the right.

'Hang on, Sir,' said Thomson, coming up from behind. But it was too late. The bay, now standing immobile in the centre of the track, turned to look at the others galloping towards them. And Carmichael slithered out of the saddle, grabbed at his horse's neck, missed, and landed face down on the soft forest floor with his right foot twisted up in the stirrup leather behind him.

Thomson jumped from his own horse, and ran over. 'You alright, Sir?' It sounded like the man was crying, and Carmichael's shoulders were heaving up and down, but when he rolled over, Thomson realised he was laughing. Thomson laughed too, releasing the lieutenant's foot from the stirrup leather.

Carmichael lay on his back and stared up at the sun above, peeping over the edge of the tree tops around them. 'I think,' he said, sitting up, 'that I will stick to aeroplanes.'

By the time Harry caught them up, Carmichael was standing alongside his horse, and patting her neck. Harry looked at Thomson, and then he looked across to Carmichael. 'So,' he said, 'that's walking, trotting, cantering and galloping covered, Sir. We only have to do jumping and you've finished your basic horsemanship test.'

*

They turned back along the track and made their way towards the junction that Carmichael had galloped past earlier. Thomson decided that walking was probably safer for now, and he followed the other two who rode abreast. They came to the turning, and Harry used his own horse to nudge the bay around the corner, and then they continued at a walking pace. 'How long have you been flying, Sir?'

'My father acquired an Avro a few years ago, part of his remuneration for investing in the company that manufactures them. A pilot flew it into the estate. I was home from school on the summer holidays and before he went back south on the train, he took me up a few times. As soon as the aircraft left the ground, I knew it was what I wanted to do.'

Harry couldn't imagine being part of a family that had its own aeroplane, much less an estate on which to keep it.

'I joined a flying club near the school and took lessons whenever I could. The Headmaster was keen; he felt it engendered an independent spirit. I joined the Royal Flying Corps as soon as I left university. They were thrilled to have someone with flying experience and the right school background. Naturally, I was delighted to get to fly at someone else's expense.'

'I'd love to go up.'

Carmichael looked over. 'I'll tell you what. If we manage to get back to our lines, I promise you a ride.'

'Really?'

Carmichael laughed at Harry's grinning face. 'Yes, I promise. After all, you've given me the opportunity of learning to ride,' he patted his horse's neck, 'so it's the least I can do, Thatcher.'

The two fell quiet again, and neither felt they could make the effort to break the silence, and so the afternoon wore on with just the sound of their passage through the forest to disturb the peace.

*

Harry realised that he could no longer so easily discern the edge of the track ahead, and glancing up, he noticed that the sun had dipped well below the treeline above.

'We probably shouldn't continue through the night,' said Thomson from behind. 'One of the horses could easily injure themselves and then we'd be buggered.'

Carmichael looked at his watch. 'Probably another hour or so of decent light. Let's keep going for now, then we'll stop and move off the track.'

Harry's stomach rumbled. 'I heard that, Thatcher. We'll split the remainder of the food, too. Hopefully, we'll find somewhere to get some food tomorrow.'

'What about the horses, Sir?'

Carmichael hadn't thought about the horses. 'What do they eat?'

'We normally have forage for them, in the transport lines,' said Harry, 'but if we can find a clearing somewhere, they'll be delighted with the grass. Water's another matter, though, for us as well as them.'

'We'll find a stream,' said Thomson.

'Let's get some more distance covered,' said Carmichael, sounding more bold than he felt.

'Will you be alright, Sir?' said Harry, looking over.

'I think I'll have to be. We must make sure we get to the southwest corner of the forest before our army has gone past.'

'Pass me your reins, Sir. I'll lead her.'

And so, for the next hour, the three trotted down the track, heading, they hoped, for a point where they would intersect with the retreating BEF before the Germans got there.

As night fell, Thomson heard gunfire in the distance: the low rumble of artillery. He was about to mention it to the others when Carmichael looked around. 'Sounds like the two armies are still in contact,' he said. 'Let's see if we can find a clearing and, with luck, water. While there's still light.'

Harry handed back Carmichael his reins. 'I'll take the lead, shall I, Sir?'

Carmichael nodded, and Harry nudged the grey to his left where he saw a gap in the treeline. He ducked to pass beneath a low branch and then began to thread his way through the trees in search of somewhere suitable, and hopefully safe, to spend the night. The others walked their mounts close behind.

*

Thomson was wrong; it wasn't artillery, but a summer storm. The rain poured into the clearing from the dark skies above, turning the ground into a mud slick. Harry led the three horses to the margin of the clearing. He secured each of them with a picket peg and they began to eat the grass at the edge of the clearing. He unfastened the blanket roll from each animal.

Walking back to where the others sheltered beneath the trees a few yards away, he handed Carmichael and Thomson each one of the blankets. 'They're a bit damp, I'm afraid, and the waterproof sheets are missing.' Carmichael threw his over his shoulders and nodded his thanks.

Harry removed the German pack and set it on the ground. He took the four water bottles and unscrewed the caps. He stepped back in the downpour and pushed each flask into the mud so that they wouldn't tip over. The rain was so bad, he knew that it wouldn't take long to fill them. He had thought about using the canvas water buckets that each horse had on its kit, but he wanted to be able to take some water with them, so the bottles must be filled.

'Good thinking, Thatcher,' said Carmichael, the blanket pulled up over his head so that he peeped from beneath its edge to see Harry.

Thomson reached into Harry's pack. He found Carmichael's Webley at the top. 'Do you want this back, Sir?'

Carmichael shook his head. 'Thatcher can keep it for now.'

Thomson handed it to Harry. 'Stick it in your haversack. Easier to get to.'

Harry nodded and opening the small bag, he pushed the handgun inside. There wasn't room to close it, so he removed his spare socks and tried again. It still wouldn't close properly, and it would hang awkwardly at his waist, but it would do.

Thomson pulled out the last of their food. He looked at the dismal collection of cheese rind, sausage skin and stale bread crust. Nevertheless, he began to carefully divide the spoils.

Harry stood, his own blanket draped over his shoulders to keep out the worst of the cold, and stared across at the three horses. They stood, heads hung, huddled as close as they could, their backs to the weather.

Finishing the few mouthfuls of his supper, Thomson took up his rifle and removed the cleaning kit from beneath the rifle's butt plate, setting it on the ground. Carmichael watched him as he removed the rifle's bolt and then released the magazine by pressing the catch beneath the trigger guard, putting them next to the cleaning kit. He lifted the rifle and held it upside down between his knees, making sure the muzzle didn't touch the ground. Then he lowered the weighted pull-through cord into the breech. It dropped easily through the barrel, and Thomson lifted the rifle, taking the pull-through weight in his fingers as it appeared at the muzzle. He pulled the cord until it came out of the barrel. Setting aside the pull-through, he began to oil the metal parts of the rifle with a small square of cloth.

Carmichael lost interest and looked over to Harry. He had wandered across to the horses again and was carefully examining each of the animal's feet, picking at their hooves with a small metal instrument, although to what end, Carmichael had no idea. The noise of Thomson working the metal parts of the rifle was very restful, and Carmichael closed his eyes.

'Here, Sir,' said Harry. Carmichael jerked upright, looked around him, and then realised that he had dropped off. He looked up, and Harry handed him one of the water bottles.

'Thank you.' Carmichael emptied the flask in a few swallows. He hadn't realised how thirsty he was. 'Maybe we should refill them?' Harry nodded and took the empty flask back into the clearing and set it on the ground.

When he stood upright, he thought he saw something across the other side of the clearing. He stared at the place where he had detected movement. A moment passed, and he decided that it had been the wind and rain thrashing a tree branch. Then he heard voices. He looked over to where Thomson and Carmichael sat huddled together. They showed no signs of alarm. He glanced across to the horses, and his breath caught in his throat as he realised the three of them were looking over towards the same spot on the far side of the clearing.

There was no doubt. They were no longer alone.

Thirteen

Harry turned slowly and began to walk back to the others. 'Someone's here.'

'What?'

'Someone else is in the clearing. Far side.' Harry pointed over his back with a thumb. Thomson and Carmichael leaned around Harry's legs and stared across. Carmichael couldn't see anyone, and was about to tell the lad he was imagining things, when he saw movement.

Thomson watched as two men stepped into the clearing, each leading a horse. Thomson inserted the rifle's bolt as softly as he could, and then pushed a round into the breech. He stood, his blanket dropping to the ground around his feet. 'Come on,' he said gripping his rifle in his right hand by its stock. 'We must get out of here.'

He edged around the clearing, keeping to the trees, and unfastened the gelding from the peg staked in the soft ground. Holding the reins, he waited for the others. 'When we go, we go together and we walk into the woods the way we came in.' He pointed to the gap in the trees behind them.

Harry began to walk into the forest leading his mare, Carmichael close behind. Thomson waited a moment, and then made to follow. There was a cry, and Thomson turned quickly, his rifle coming up to his shoulder. He saw three indistinct figures in the murk at the far side of the clearing. One was pointing towards Thomson, and another had his rifle butt to his shoulder. The third was swinging up into his saddle.

Thomson didn't hesitate and squeezed the trigger. The bullet caught the distant rifleman in his head, and he crumpled to the ground. More horsemen came into the clearing at the sound of the shot, ducking beneath low branches heavy with rain. Thomson dropped to his knee and aimed again, firing once more. The finger pointer staggered and then fell back, releasing his reins and his horse trotted away from his body and stopped a few yards further on.

'Get out of there, Thomson,' said Carmichael from somewhere behind.

Thomson stood up, stuck his foot into the left stirrup and, ignoring the bullets whipping into the forest around him, he mounted the black horse. Once on its back, he kicked him on, and then turned in the saddle. A German cavalryman was across the clearing, his lance at the ready. He was no more than three horse lengths behind. Beyond him, Thomson saw other enemy horsemen spurring forwards. He swung his rifle one-handed and pointed the muzzle at the approaching German. He squeezed the trigger and he was lucky: the bullet struck the enemy cavalryman in the chest. His lance point dropped, his horse slowed to a trot and then came to a halt. Thomson fired twice more at the other horsemen before the forest swallowed him up.

A few yards further on, he saw the dim shapes of his companions, and the three began to trot through the trees. There were loud shouts from behind them, and wild firing in their direction. Bullets clipped the tree trunks and sliced through foliage.

A branch smacked Harry in his face, soaking his tunic with rain water, and he ducked lower. He could hear a commotion not far behind as the enemy attempted to follow their trail. He knew they couldn't be seen, but a random shot could kill just as easily as an aimed one, and so he kicked his horse on, pressing his body low to her neck as she sought a way through the tangle of trees.

The grey seemed to know what to do and she ran between the trunks of the trees, somehow managing to avoid the lowest branches. Harry glanced over his shoulder, saw movement further back and knew they were after him still. He kicked again at the mare's sides, urging her on, but she knew her business.

Suddenly, Harry broke through the undergrowth and found himself standing in one of the hunting lanes. He looked up and down the track, but there was no sign of the other two. He was alone.

A shout made him turn in the saddle. He wasn't alone; a hundred yards away, three German cavalrymen burst from the forest, shouting as they caught sight of their quarry. They cantered forward, lances coming down, and Harry froze, staring at his approaching death.

*

When the first enemy horseman was no more than twenty yards away, Harry heaved on the reins, pulling the mare to face the attack. His hand dropped to his right, and he grasped the sword's grip, pulling it from the scabbard in one smooth motion.

The German leaned from his saddle, and he tensed his arm and upper body, ready to drive the lance through the British trooper. Harry's sword came across his body, and he nudged the grey to his left as he continued the swing of the steel blade. It struck the shaft of the lance, slicing off a chunk of wood as the German shot past, deflecting the lance tip.

Harry spurred on, leaving the first horseman behind turning in the track to come up behind Harry. Up ahead, the other two rode abreast, and Harry knew he would have to pass between them. They knew it too, and knew that he could not deflect both lances.

Harry switched the sword to his left hand and reached down to his haversack. He was suddenly glad that he had been unable to fasten it. He brought up Carmichael's pistol and aimed it at the horseman on the left. The Germans saw the weapon, and accelerated towards Harry, hoping to kill him before the pistol could fire; they were too late.

The Webley kicked hard in Harry's hand as he squeezed the trigger, and a bullet struck the horseman on the right. He veered to the side of the track, his lance forgotten as he clutched his wounded arm. Harry fired again, driving the grey mare to the right hand side of the track, a gap opening between the two enemy horses. The second bullet disappeared into the forest, and then Harry was up to the enemy horseman. The German leaned across his horse's head to bring his lance to the target. Harry yanked with desperation at his reins, and the grey stopped.

The German couldn't change his position in the saddle quickly enough, and his lance tip struck the hand guard of Harry's sword, knocking Harry's left arm hard back. The

German swung around, Harry kicked the mare, and she took off up the track, passing the wounded horseman.

Feeling like a cowboy from a Western film, Harry turned in the saddle and fired the Webley at the Germans following him. He pushed the pistol back into his haversack and then took the sword in his right hand, his left arm numb from the impact with the lance.

He looked back again. The enemy were still after him and closing the gap. Harry searched ahead for another junction or a gap in the trees, but he could see nothing in the dim light. Glancing behind, he realised that they had closed the gap and would be on him in moments. He knew he must turn and face them.

He pulled the reins, turning the mare towards the threat, and then he stood with his sword resting across the saddle while he tried to think. There was nothing for it. He squeezed the mare's flanks, and she responded, running towards the galloping enemy.

Time appeared to slow, and Harry's senses took on a clarity he had never known before. He noticed that the horseman on the right had an unlit cigar clamped between his teeth. He saw a small bird, disturbed by their passage, fly from a tree branch to safety higher up. He realised that the second horseman had his top three tunic buttons unfastened.

Harry straightened his arm, locking his elbow and selected the easier target; the man on his right. He knew he could not kill them both, but he could try to get one. The man on the left stiffened in his saddle, arching his back. Harry watched his head extend and then his face disappear into a burst of red. And then Harry struck the remaining horseman, his blade sliding along the wooden shaft of the lance. His sword tip struck the German in his right shoulder, slicing through muscle and rendering the arm useless.

Harry was past, and up ahead, two more horsemen, one with a rifle to his shoulder. There was a flash, and Harry expected to feel the bullet, but there was nothing. The horseman ahead lowered his rifle, and then Harry knew who they were.

'Where have you been, lad?'

Harry looked back. The two enemy cavalrymen lay dead on the track, their horses standing by their bodies. He turned and grinned at Thomson and Carmichael. 'I must have got lost.' And then the adrenalin caught up with him, and he retched, the water he had drunk earlier splashing onto his horse's shoulder.

Thomson looked around, aware that there would be more enemy troops somewhere in the woods, and they would have been alerted by his rifle shots. As he watched Harry push the sword blade back into his scabbard and then wipe his mouth, Thomson took a clip of ammunition and reloaded his rifle. 'Right, if you've finished playing, Thatcher, it's time for us to get going.'

Slotting his rifle into the leather bucket, Thomson lead the three of them forward. They passed the two dead Germans, and Harry couldn't bring himself to look down at them. 'It was you or them, Thatcher,' said Thomson. 'You or them.'

They had no idea in which direction they were going, but they continued on for twenty minutes or so. Then Thomson held up a hand and stopped. He tipped his head on one side, straining to hear above the noise of the rain, listening for sounds of pursuit. After a moment or two, he nodded and the three continued. They soon came to a junction with another forest track.

Carmichael looked left and right, but without a compass, a map or even the stars to guide them, he had no idea which way to go. He turned to the others. 'We'll wait for morning. Soon as we see the sun, we'll be on our way. Till then, we should move off this track.'

'Won't be long. I can already see better than before. Dawn can't be far away.' Thomson looked over to Harry. 'What have you done to your face, Thatcher?'

Harry lifted his hand again; felt the sticky wetness. 'Tree branch. Don't think it's serious.'

'I could do with a drink of water,' said Thomson.

Harry hesitated. 'I left the bottles in the clearing,' he said at last. 'Along with the German pack.'

'Well, that should confuse them,' said Carmichael. 'With luck, they might think they just opened fire on their own troops. Let's get off this track.'

*

They reached the south-western end of the forest without encountering any more German troops. Harry tethered the horses a little way back, hidden by the shadows of the trees, and the three crept forward. They knelt, huddled close together, and stared out across the fields beyond the forest.

The line of guns fired again, one after the other. German guns, firing indirectly at targets to the southwest. Carmichael glanced to the left. The sun was just above the horizon, and looking forwards, he wondered how on earth they were to get past the German First Army, vast units of which now stood between them and the BEF further south. 'Ideas?'

Thomson studied the area around them; took in the long, straight Roman road running past the western face of the forest in a roughly southerly direction. It passed within two miles of them off to their right. He pointed at it. 'That's where our lads will have gone.'

'I don't see much chance of us getting through all this. We might have to wait until nightfall again.'

'But surely there will be more German troops around this area by then, Sir?' said Harry, the feeling of hopelessness suddenly overwhelming.

'Maybe we should head east and look for the flank of the German army, and try to get around the back of them?' said Thomson. 'Or even west?'

'Wait here.' Carmichael crept out from between the close growing trees and walked a few yards further before dropping to his knees and looking south. He could see that the forest continued almost to a village. After staring south for a couple of minutes, he walked back to the others.

'If we ride to the southern tip of the forest, there's a village no more than three or four hundred yards beyond the last of the trees. How long does it take a galloping horse to cover four hundred yards?'

'A blooming long time if someone's shooting at you all the while,' said Thomson.

'It's probably our only chance; to continue wandering the rear area of the advancing German army is to invite capture. Or worse.'

'Capture's better than being dead, Sir,' said Thomson.

'I suppose I could order you both to comply, but we've come this far without recourse to military discipline. What do you think? Are you both game?'

Harry took a few steps forward and looked south. He could see where the forest came to an abrupt end and, sure enough, there were some houses visible just beyond. He thought about getting back to the Regiment; about seeing his brother again. He turned to look at the others. 'I'm game, Sir.'

'Thomson?'

Thomson looked at Harry and then at Carmichael. 'Yes, alright.'

*

'There must be two regiments in front of us. At least.' Thomson was beginning to regret agreeing to Carmichael's hell for leather, all or nothing plan.

'Yes, but that's the British beyond; in the village. I suggest we try to walk our horses down the road that leads to the village and if we're challenged, we just gallop.'

'That's your plan, is it, Sir?'

'Yes. I can't think of anything better.'

Harry stared out of the trees at the German infantry. They were lying in hastily cut scrapes in the dirt facing the village. Beyond them, Harry was sure he could detect the movement of troops behind barricades of heaped furniture and along low walls that bordered the houses on the edge of the small town; presumably British, or maybe French troops. He looked to the right, and stretching into the distance, there were men in field-grey uniforms advancing towards the village.

'Right, then.' Thomson unsheathed his rifle and checked it was fully loaded. He returned it to the bucket, and then he went around the black gelding checking the tack, making sure all was tight and fastened where it should be. 'Wouldn't do to fall off because of a loose stirrup leather,' he said to Carmichael with a smile.

After Thomson had checked his own horse, he did the same for Carmichael's, and there being no further reason to delay, he swung up into the saddle and looked down at the other two. 'Right, then,' he said again.

Harry mounted and the mare could sense his excitement; perhaps she could smell his fear? She moved from foot to foot, unable to stand still. When Carmichael had finally managed to get into his saddle, Thomson said: 'I think I should lead, with Harry bringing up the rear.'

'No, I shall take the lead.'

'With respect, Sir, you know nothing about using a sword, and it might just come to hacking our way through.'

'I'll have you know, I was runner-up in the fencing championships at school; two years running.'

'Runner-up won't count for much today, Sir.'

Carmichael blinked and then nodded.

'Right, then,' said Thomson, unaware that his repetition gave away his own fear. He clicked his tongue and nudged the gelding with his heels, and the big horse strolled out into the morning sunlight. Thomson immediately felt exposed by the sudden lack of surrounding trees, but he walked steadily on.

Carmichael followed a few feet behind, with Harry at the back. As they advanced, Harry felt like he imagined you would when walking down the High Street naked. He kept his eyes forwards and dared not look around him.

They had managed to go about a hundred yards when a German NCO in charge of a section of two field guns caught sight of the three horsemen. He waved over at them, and then, frowning, he called out.

Thomson ignored the man, but watched him from the corner of his eyes. The man shouted something again, and Thomson saw a few of the nearest gun crew turn and watch their advance. He squeezed his calves and the gelding responded instantly, coming to the gallop as if a button had been pressed.

Carmichael, who had also been watching the German sergeant, found the gap between himself and Thomson opening wide before he could react. But then his horse responded for him; seeing her companion galloping away, she pulled at the reins curled through Carmichael's hands, and was off in pursuit.

Harry's stomach tightened and the fear threatened to bring him down, but he followed his training and let the grey run. She was a hand shorter than Thomson's mount, but she was fast, and she closed the gap quickly, passing Carmichael with ease.

The German sergeant stood with his hands on his hips, somewhat confused by the reaction to his question. And then it dawned on him, and he turned to the crew of the field guns and shouted across to them. There were enemy horsemen to their rear, and the men grabbed at their rifles and sent a couple of shots at the departing horses.

Up ahead, Thomson saw there was a gap in the enemy line where one regiment finished and another began; a gap of only a couple of yards, but he turned towards it. He could see a few heads turning to look back as he galloped down towards them. Alarmed faces, rifles coming around, and then the first few bullets whistled close to Thomson's head. His horse stumbled, and he thought they would go down, but the gelding kept to his feet.

Thomson drew his sword, the blade grating in the scabbard as it came free. He was within yards of the enemy line, coming at them from behind. Two men stood in the gap, their rifles at their shoulders. Thomson nudged the horse to the left, and as he flashed through the gap, he crashed into one man, sending him head over heels backwards. Turning to his right as he passed, he brought the heavy, steel blade down in an arc that ended in a thud as it struck the remaining enemy infantryman in his neck. Blood, bright arterial blood, sheeted over the dry grass. But Thomson was through and back low in the saddle, the sword held upright almost at the salute.

Harry passed through the gap just as the second German fell, and the mare leapt, clearing the dying man without hesitation. Harry looked back over his shoulder, saw Carmichael coming between the two regiments, and then he looked forward to Thomson. He couldn't see him for a moment, and then he realised that he had passed behind one of the tall corn stooks that stood sentinel in the field. There he was again, approaching the village. Harry was catching him, now, the black gelding slowing. At the back of Harry's mind, the sudden thought that they might now be brought down not by the enemy, but by the British riflemen he could see crowding the walls and barricades ahead.

Carmichael saw Thomson's big horse leap the wall and then he disappeared into a garden beyond. He had fretted about his skill in the saddle being up to the challenge of keeping pace, but the bay had wanted nothing other than to catch up with her companions and she leapt the surprised enemy infantry in her desire to do just that.

Harry watched Thomson sail over the low wall into the garden beyond, knew he would be telling the defenders to hold their fire; that a British cavalry patrol was coming in. And then the wall was there, and he stared down into the eyes of the defenders; friendly eyes, khaki caps above them. Harry came up in his stirrups, lifting his backside off the saddle, and she sailed easily above the low wall. Men dived out of their way as he sought to bring her to a standstill.

The grey was blowing hard, but Harry was already out of the saddle and turning to look back. And there was Carmichael, a look of utter terror on his face as his horse carried him over the wall like a sack of coal. He had leaned back as the horse had come up, and both his feet came out of the stirrups, but they landed lightly, and the mare stopped as quick as she could. With nothing holding him to the horse, Carmichael, still unbalanced, continued over the mare's head and landed in a heap at Harry's feet.

'You alright, Sir?'

'Remind me never to take to the saddle again, Thatcher. Ever.' Carmichael sat up and smiled.

But they had done it. They had got back to their lines.

Fourteen

'Where the hell did you three come from?' said a captain.

Harry stood up and saluted, opened his mouth to speak, then changed his mind and looked down at Carmichael for help.

'We got separated from our units, Sir,' said Carmichael, getting to his feet. 'In my case, by quite a way.'

'Right, well, you can help here. We could do with every available man.' The captain glanced to the wall behind which the men of his company knelt defending the edge of the village.

'Thatcher, deal with the horses and then get back here,' said Carmichael.

Harry nodded. He took the bay mare by the reins and led her over to his own grey who stood idly munching on a patch of dried grass at the edge of a road that led through the centre of the village. He walked the two horses on a bit and, finding Thomson standing with his black gelding near a large house, he tethered the two of them to a tree in the garden.

The front door of the house stood open, and through it, Harry could see papers and books scattered across the polished wooden flooring. Halfway up the garden path leading to the door, an old, brown leather suitcase lay open, ladies' undergarments spilling across the limestone paving. Whoever lived there had left in a hurry, thought Harry.

'Expensive looking undies.'

Harry nodded and pulled out his rifle.

'More action?' said Thomson, his own slung over his shoulder.

'Looks like it.' The two began to walk back to the edge of the village.

'You two. On the double,' yelled a sergeant, spotting them as they rounded the end of the last house in the village. They ran up, and the sergeant pushed them up to the wall. 'You cavalry lads know how to shoot, right?' he said. Harry knew better than to answer, and he turned to the wall, and resting his rifle on the bricks, he looked along the sights. He could see the point two hundred yards away where they had cut through the enemy line and he adjusted the backsight for that distance.

'I shouldn't bother with aiming, son,' said the sergeant. 'They'll be climbing over the wall before the hour's out. And where's your bayonet?'

'They don't give us a bayonet, Sergeant.'

'Probably afraid they'll hurt themselves with it,' said one of the defending infantry, grinning at his mates.

'Yes, probably,' said Thomson. 'They do give us a 35 inch sword, though. How long's your little thing?'

The infantryman grunted and turned to face out once more.

Thomson's eyes caught the movement of what he assumed was an officer moving behind the prone enemy soldiers, probably passing on orders or giving encouragement. He took aim, slowed his breathing, and then when he was ready, he held his breath on the exhale. He squeezed the trigger rather than pulled it, and the bullet crossed the two hundred yards to his target in a quarter of a second, striking the German officer in his throat. The sound of the shot reached the officer's ears a quarter second later, but he was already going backwards. The bullet sliced through his neck and severed the spinal cord before spinning upwards and entering his brain. He was dead before his brain could register the sound of the shot.

A bullet struck the wall next to Thomson's face, a puff of pink brick dust marking its passing. He ignored it, and pulled the rifle bolt up, back, and then slotted it forward and down, loading another round from the magazine. He selected another target: a man lying in a shallow trench, his head and shoulders just visible. He was no different to any of the other five hundred men lying two hundred yards away, but he was the one Thomson had chosen.

The second of Thomson's bullets struck the intended target, a young man from a farm near Magdeburg in central Germany. It shattered his collar bone and scraped along the inside of his shoulder blade before passing along the length of his body, just beneath his ribs. The regimental surgeon would later remove the bullet from the man's right buttock.

There was a distant cry, and as one, the German infantry came to their feet and began to run forwards. Thomson fired again and again. The man to Harry's left fell back without a sound. Looking down, Harry could see a small hole in the man's forehead. He pulled the trigger and sent a bullet into the mass of enemy troops, but he'd no idea whether he had hit anyone. He reloaded and fired again.

The enemy infantrymen sought cover as they advanced, crouching behind the corn stooks to fire at the British defenders before coming to their feet and advancing again. Harry watched, and realised that they were working in groups: one provided covering fire as another ran forward. The garden echoed to the sharp crack of rifle fire as the British defenders poured fifteen to twenty aimed shots each across at the attackers. Fearsome gunfire, but Harry could see it would not be enough to hold back the hordes of field-grey figures.

As if reading his thoughts, the captain spoke from behind him. 'We're pulling back again, lads. We're going to make a fighting withdrawal along the road that heads south. The field artillery will provide us some cover, and then when they withdraw, we'll cover them. Sergeant? I'll leave you here with Johnson's platoon. Give us a couple of minutes, and then get after us.'

'Come on, Thatcher,' said Thomson. 'Time to get going again.' Turning, Harry spotted Carmichael beyond the infantry captain in the road that led through the village. They ran over. 'Time to go, Sir,' said Harry, and the three ran up the street to where the horses waited.

Harry stopped in his tracks and stared at the tree by the house with the underwear in the garden. The black gelding was lying across the garden path, his head held up by the rope attached to the tree. There was blood visible at his nose and across the dirt in front of his body.

Thomson knelt. 'Must have caught a bullet on the way in,' he said, raising a bloodied hand. No one spoke for a moment.

'Right,' said Carmichael. 'Time for me to seek alternative travel arrangements, I think.'

'Hold on, Sir. Why don't you come with us; at least as far as the next village. If we leave you here, you'll get caught.'

'But we're short a horse, Thatcher, and I did vow to stay off the wretched things.'

Harry looked down the road towards the lightly defended barricade at the northern tip of the village. 'We can both ride the grey. We're not going far.'

Carmichael stood at the side of the street, British troops streaming back behind him, firing back as they ran. They were making their way to the southern end of the village where they would turn and provide covering fire for the rest of their company. He knew Harry was right. 'Alright. So long as you're the one in charge of the horse.'

With Thomson watching, amused, from the back of the bay mare, Carmichael struggled to get onto the grey. Eventually, he managed it, and with his arms tight around Harry's waist, and struggling to keep his dignity, the three of them trotted up the road, the infantry staring up at them with envy as they passed.

*

No sooner had the British infantry left the cover of the wall at the northern end of the village than the Germans began to swarm forward. The sergeant shouted to the remaining men of the platoon under his command, and they fell back, still firing. When they rounded the bend in the road where the black gelding lay dead, they began to run up the road.

The sound of small arms fire was suddenly loud, echoing along the street. Carmichael looked around in alarm and saw the running British infantry. 'Come on, Thatcher, get a move on.'

Harry dug his heels into the mare's sides, and she broke into a canter. They reached the far end of the village. The bulk of the British infantry were beyond the village by some two hundred yards, taking up defensive positions. And beyond them, Harry saw horse drawn artillery coming up. His spirits rose. Could Richard be amongst the crews? He watched the horses being turned quickly, bringing the guns around. Men leapt down from the gun and the ammunition limber and moments later, the horses were ridden off to safety beyond the hill.

Harry and Thomson cleared the end of the village, the last of the British defenders just behind them. They cantered up the gentle slope towards the waiting British guns. Harry stared at the men of the gun sections as they readied them for action: ammunition was carried closer to the guns, and the fuze set for the very short distance to target; the major commanding the battery ran between each gun, checking that it was aimed correctly and at the right elevation.

'The Germans are at this end of the village, Thatcher,' said Carmichael. Harry glanced around, and then pulling at the bit, he urged the grey to a sharp right turn. 'Steady on.' Carmichael tightened his grip around Harry's waist.

'They're about to open fire, Sir. Look.'

Carmichael stared up the hill, and he saw that the crews of the guns were kneeling behind their weapons, ready. And then the first fired over the heads of the British infantry further down the slope, and the six shrapnel shells burst almost simultaneously at the southern end of the village, shredding the advancing German infantry.

Ten seconds later, the guns fired again, a little more raggedly than before, as each team reloaded at a different rate. Harry turned his horse and he and Carmichael stared back at the village. Blood stained the road. Germans were trying to get clear of the hail of shrapnel from the British shells, seeking cover behind garden walls, trees, anywhere they could find.

Harry watched one German soldier, struggling under the weight of a fallen comrade. He had his friend over his shoulder and was staggering back towards the village in the hopes of finding safety. The guns fired a third time, and the man and his wounded comrade went down and did not get up again.

'Come on, Thatcher. We must catch up with Thomson.'

Harry wheeled around, and he walked the mare up the hill. The gun line was to their left, and he looked over.

'Looking for someone?'

'My brother, Sir.'

'I didn't know your brother was in the cavalry, Thatcher.'

'L Battery, Royal Horse Artillery, Sir. He's not there. Looks like 18 pounders. Royal Field Artillery guns, I think.'

The guns fired again, and Harry tried to not think about the enemy infantry caught in the open below. Thomson waited for them just beyond the crest of the hill and as they approached, he turned, and the two horses walked side by side, heading southwest towards the Roman road that slashed across the recently harvested fields.

*

'Where the hell are they all going?' said Thomson, frustrated by the constant long delays on the road.

'It's been like this since last week,' said Carmichael. 'When I was first over here, the local populace were streaming into France from all over Belgium, and I suppose these are they.'

As far as they could see, the road ahead was clogged by soldiers, horse drawn transport limbers, the occasional motor vehicle, but most of all, by tens of thousands of civilians, struggling along on foot under the weight of their possessions.

Harry looked down and his eyes met those of a British soldier. The man sat at the edge of the road, his boots off. The man's socks were dark with dried blood, and Harry turned away when he attempted to remove one of his socks, peeling a sticky layer of skin from his heel.

'You got any water, chum?' said another man from the other side of the road. Harry turned at the voice. Two infantrymen sat in the meagre shade of a small tree just off the road. 'Water?' said one of them again, his face burnt red, the skin on his lips cracked dry by the fierce sun. Harry shook his head. He hadn't had anything to drink himself since before dawn, and didn't need reminding.

The column came to another halt. Men and women sat where they had stood, some using their suitcases as chairs, others just dropping to the ground, delighted for the rest, and patiently waiting for the way ahead to clear. Harry noticed that there was little fuss being made by the children that made up a fair proportion of the fleeing civilians. He guessed that their total exhaustion had rendered them silent.

Thomson moved to the edge of the road and urged his horse down the short drop to the field beyond. 'We'll be quicker this way,' he said. Thatcher followed, and they began to make steady progress, overhauling those that remained on the road.

Fifty yards further along, the cause of the delay was obvious. A horse had died. The driver of the limber was working quickly to cut the animal from the traces, and then he and half a dozen other men dragged the horse clear, pushing him in a tangle of stiff limbs down the verge. There was a further delay as the driver climbed back in and urged the remaining horse on.

Harry and the others rode on through the heat of midday, and on into the afternoon, barely speaking. Around mid-afternoon, Harry cried out. 'Look,' he said, staring over to their left. Carmichael raised himself from his stupor and glanced across the fields. Thomson turned his head to follow Harry's outstretched hand, and in the distance, he could see horsemen cantering past, although of what nationality, he couldn't tell.

'Should we join them?'

Thomson shook his head. 'They could be anyone. We should wait until we're sure it's a British unit.'

A roar grew behind them, and lifting his eyes away from the departing horsemen, Carmichael looked up just as an aircraft flashed by overhead. 'One of ours,' he said, recognising the aircraft type. 'Lucky devils.' He knew that they would be eating in the mess that night while he and the others would still be on the road. He closed his eyes against the glare of the sun off the dirt at the side of the road, and after a few moments, Harry felt Carmichael's head nudge his back as he fell asleep. He lifted a hand from the reins and gripped Carmichael's tunic cuff; he didn't want him to fall off.

And they rode on, and the snake of refugees and retreating soldiers walked stoically through the worst of the afternoon's heat. And Harry tried to think about anything but a drink of water.

*

The rain came in the early evening. Harry tipped his head back and let the water run into his mouth. It wasn't much, but it was delightful. Carmichael jerked suddenly awake as the rain went down his tunic collar and soaked his back.

'Alright, Lieutenant?'

'How long was I asleep?'

'Couple of hours, Sir.'

'Where are we?' Carmichael looked around him. Indistinct in the rain, he could see the refugees on the road twenty yards or so distant.

'We've been plodding along the same road all day, Sir. I've no idea where we're going, but I hope we get there soon.'

'I need to stop.'

'Yes, Sir. Thomson?'

Thomson looked over, nodded, and edged closer. There was a distant flash on the horizon, and then a few seconds later, a heavy peal of thunder.

'I need a break, Thomson. Perhaps up yonder by those trees?' Carmichael pointed ahead.

'Sir.' Thomson sheared away and was swallowed by the dark and rain. Moments later, Harry saw him swing his leg over the rear of the saddle and jump down. He staggered, exhaustion threatening to overcome him, and then taking the mare's reins, he led her away from the road into the partial respite from the rain offered by the line of plane trees that bordered the road.

Harry pulled up his own mount. 'You get off first, Sir.'

Carmichael grasped both sides of Harry's wet tunic, and then tried to bring his right leg up and over the back of the horse. He slipped, grabbed at the saddle, and slid to the ground.

'You really must work on the dismount, Sir,' said Thomson, smiling.

Carmichael got to his feet. The seat of his trousers were sopping wet, and he nodded to Thomson before walking quickly to the treeline.

Harry stood next to Thomson and the two watched their adopted officer as he pulled down his trousers and leaned back against one of the tree trunks. After a moment, they saw him pull something from his tunic pocket. It looked to Harry like a book, and Carmichael busied himself ripping pages from it and wiping them between his buttocks.

He stood and pulled up his breeches, fastening the buttons and then straightening his tunic. He walked back with as much dignity as the situation would allow. Neither Harry nor Thomson spoke for a moment, and then Thomson said: 'Better, Sir?'

Carmichael held up the book. 'I knew this would come in useful.'

'What is it?'

'A bible; a gift from a maternal aunt when we left for France.'

Harry's mouth fell open.

Thomson looked at the bible and then glanced across to the trees. 'May I, Sir?' he said, putting out a hand.

'For if people do these things when the tree is green, what will happen when it is dry?'

'Pardon, Sir?'

'Luke 23-31.' Carmichael placed the depleted bible into Thomson's hand. 'You surely attended Sunday School, Trooper?'

'Never missed it, Sir,' said Thomson as he walked towards the trees.

A moment later, the lighting flashed again, illuminating Thomson crouched behind one of the other trees, bible at the ready.

'It's not really a bible, Thatcher.'

'No, Sir?'

Carmichael shook his head. 'It's an anthology of dull poetry: Byron, mostly, Shelley; that kind of thing. Though it was a gift from an aunt.'

'I am relieved, Sir. I did think that in our present situation, we were pushing our luck with the Almighty.'

'Because the army's grown more popular, At which the naval people are concern'd,' said Carmichael as the two watched Thomson walking back towards them.

'Don Juan, Sir?'

Carmichael turned and looked at Harry. 'That's twice you've surprised me, young Thatcher. Once with the German guard and now with your knowledge of what surely must be the world's longest poem.'

'Shall we get going, Sir?' said Thomson, handing back the book.

'It's rather thinner than when we stopped.' Carmichael raised an eyebrow and pushed the book into his tunic pocket.

'Sorry about that, Sir. Got the runs, I'm afraid.'

'Thank you, Thomson. Please do feel free to keep us apprised of your bowel movements,' said Carmichael as Harry helped him back up onto their horse.

'I will, Sir,' said Thomson, and he clicked his tongue and urged his mare to a trot to catch the other two.

Fifteen

'There's a town up ahead, Sir,' said Harry over his shoulder. 'Quite big, by the looks of it.'

Carmichael stirred himself. He'd spent the rest of the night huddled against the young trooper's back, trying to keep warm despite being wet through. The storm had abated during the night and then died away at dawn. He looked around Harry's shoulders. 'Probably Saint-Quentin,' he said, spotting the cathedral.

'Might be able to find something to eat; for us, and the horses,' said Thomson, riding just behind them.

They rode down the main street towards the town square, the civilians grumbling as they forced through the throng.

'Look. It's Major Allen.' Harry twisted from left to right, scanning the streets that led into the square, searching for the rest of their regiment.

Major Allen was standing in front of a large gathering of British infantry, few of whom were standing. They lay in careless attitudes, their rifles stacked, delighted to have escaped the following Germans, at least for a while.

'Look, you men,' Allen was saying, 'you'd surely not want to spend the war in a prison camp? Come with me.'

A corporal with a week's dark growth on his face, came to his feet and stepped towards the major. 'Listen. We've had a bellyful of fighting and running. Our officers have said we're to surrender and that's fine with us.'

There was a murmur of approval from the soldiers around his feet.

'And,' the corporal continued, bolstered by the support of his mates, 'we don't need no interfering twit from the cavalry sticking his nose in where it's not wanted.'

Major Allen reached down to his holster.

'Oh, no you don't.' The snick of the loading of a rifle stopped the major.

'We're not moving from here, and that's final.' The corporal sat back down. The soldier with the loaded rifle on his right slapped him on the back. 'Well said, Snedley,' said another, handing the corporal a cigarette.

Allen turned on his heels and it was then he spotted the approaching horses.

'Is that you, Trooper Thomson? And young Thatcher with you?'

'It is, Sir.' Thomson grinned at his squadron commander as he swung down from the saddle.

'I was sure you two had been killed up at the sugar factory.'

'We managed to keep one step ahead of Jerry, Sir. Thanks to the Lieutenant here.'

'Carmichael,' said Carmichael, his hand outstretched. Major Allen shook it.

'What about Lieutenant Smith?'

Harry looked to Thomson. 'Dead, Sir.'

No one spoke for a moment.

'Where's the rest of the Regiment, Sir?'

'I don't know, Thatcher. I got separated at Le Cateau. Lost my horse, too. I managed to get a lift with some transport chaps, and we ended up here. Just in time to see the GHQ folk boarding a train.' He indicated the corporal and the other infantrymen with a sideways movement of his head. 'That probably explains their reluctance to keep fighting. Can't be easy when you've just seen the General staff heading south.'

Thomson stared across at the corporal and the man who had threatened his officer by loading his rifle. He would sort them both if he got the chance.

'Thomson, stay here and look to your horses. Thatcher and I will go and find their officers and see about this surrender.'

Carmichael turned to Thomson. 'I'm going to try to find some transport out of here,' he said. 'If there's a station, maybe there will be another train?'

Thomson nodded and walked the two horses across the square to the shade in front of a large hotel. A line of arches ran across the front of the hotel, and he used the horses' head ropes to secure them to the central upright. He looked around. He'd no idea where he could find forage and water for them, but he must look.

Then, across the square, he spotted a shop front. He had an idea. He couldn't understand the wording above the door but, by the pots, pans and fire irons standing in the window, he knew it was what he wanted. He stood at the side of the bay mare, withdrew Carmichael's enormous shotgun and, watched by the sullen troops in the square, he crossed to the shop and pushed open the door.

*

'There they are,' said Allen, marching at speed towards two men sitting in the shade of the veranda that surrounded a large brick-built residence. Allen saluted, but Harry hung back.

'What can we do for you, Major?' said one of the officers.

'Colonel, your men tell me that you have surrendered?'

The two officers shared a look. 'That is indeed correct, Major,' said the second officer, turning to stare at the cavalry officer.

'May I ask why?'

The first man stood. 'I am not in the habit of explaining myself to junior officers, Major.'

'These are rather exceptional circumstances, Sir. We have the Germans no more than ten or fifteen miles behind us, and we must continue to fall back. Surrender seems … precipitate,' said Allen with considerably more tact than he felt.

'You know nothing of our situation here,' said the second officer. 'I lost well over half my battalion at Le Cateau, and since then, we have been chased from pillar to post, with men getting lost along the way.'

'The Mayor will not help to equip our men,' said the other officer, indicating the house with his thumb, 'nor find them food and drink. We have no choice.'

'There is always a choice,' said Allen. 'I will see the Mayor and get your men the food they need.'

'As you will,' said the first officer, taking his seat again. 'As you will.'

Allen did not salute the two colonels, but simply turned and waved Harry over. 'Come on, lad, I'll need your French again.'

Allen walked into the hallway of the mayoral house. He could hear voices from beyond a door at the rear. Harry hurried to keep up as his officer strode through the large house, his spurs clicking on the shining floor tiles. Allen's anger with the British officers threatened to overcome him and, arriving at the closed kitchen door, he simply kicked it open.

A middle-aged man, a napkin tucked into his shirt collar, sat at a table opposite an old woman. Allen could see roasted meats, a bowl of fruit and oven-fresh bread on the table. A bowl of what smelt like onion soup sat in front of the man and woman. The man turned at the sound of the kitchen door crashing into the tiled wall and he dropped his spoon in surprise.

'You, Sir? What is the meaning of this surrender? The Germans are nowhere near us yet. We must feed our men and then get back on the road. At some point, we shall be ready to turn on our attackers. What we do not need is cowardly idiots getting in our way, Sir!'

Harry spoke as quickly as he could, translating the major's angry tirade as best as he could, selecting a more tactful phrase than *cowardly idiots*, but from the colour of the Mayor's cheeks, Harry knew that he'd understood the tone of the major's speech. He spluttered his anger, came to his feet, and began to shout back.

'What's he saying, Thatcher?'

'He says it's his town, Sir, and he will help whom he wants. He says he has no quarrel with the Germans, and that our presence here is a danger to him and his people.'

The Mayor flourished a piece of paper and waved it in Major Allen's face. Harry saw the major's hands tighten and for a moment, he thought his officer would strike the Frenchman.

'What is that?' said Allen, mastering his fury.

'He says it's the surrender document, Sir. Signed by both the colonels. He says it's all legal, Sir, and that we must also surrender.'

'I'll be damned if I will.' Allen grabbed the surrender document from the Mayor's hand and left the kitchen. The Mayor stared after him, and then began shouting again, following Harry as they left the front of the house.

Allen stood in front of the two exhausted officers. He felt some pity for them, they were plainly utterly demoralised and physically exhausted. But Allen had his duty. 'You are a disgrace to the uniform that you wear. This document shall see you damned for laying down your arms in the face of the enemy,' said Allen, holding the surrender document up, before folding it carefully and slipping it into a pocket. 'I promise you.'

With that, he and Thatcher walked away, leaving the two officers and the Mayor standing on the veranda staring after them.

*

'I noticed a toy shop on the way here, Thatcher.'

'Yes, Sir.'

'I think we can get those lads back on their feet with a little encouragement.'

'Yes, Sir.' Harry had no idea how a toy shop would help get four hundred soldiers on their feet again.

'Ah, here it is.'

There was no one inside the shop, the proprietor presumably having fled. Allen walked around, looking for something. Harry watched him from the door.

'Here we are.' Allen held up a tin trumpet. He continued his search and, after another moment, he held up a red toy drum and a penny whistle. 'I am sure that even Trooper Thomson can manage one or other of these. Come on.'

They walked back into the square and crossed towards the hotel where Thomson was busy with the horses.

'Where did you find him, Thomson?' said Allen.

The three stood around a large, grey stallion.

'He was standing in a field, Sir, and so I thought he could do with some company.'

'He's magnificent.'

'I also found some hay, Sir.'

'Well done, Thomson.'

'I've no saddle, Sir, but I can get a piece of rope and make a bit from the hardware store over yonder.' Thomson pointed to the shop he had visited earlier.

'Don't trouble yourself, Thomson. I shall manage for now.' Allen patted the big percheron's neck and then turned to stare at the men in the square. There was ribald laughter and shouting. Allen knew the signs; like Saturday night outside Tidworth barracks. They may not have found any food, but the British Tommy had an unerring nose for alcohol. He lowered his hand for his pistol, hesitated, and then changing his mind, gave the toy trumpet to Harry.

Harry pressed each of the keys tentatively. He smiled. It would do, so long as they didn't need to play anything complicated.

'And this is for you, Thomson.'

Thomson took the whistle from the major and put it to his lips. He gave it an experimental blow. It was shrill, but loud.

'Anything I can do to help?'

They turned at the voice.

'Can you play an instrument, Lieutenant?'

'I can play the piano, Sir.'

'Well, that's not going to be much bloody good today. Anything smaller?'

'I can carry a tune, Sir.' He smiled, remembering something. 'Back at school, I played Figaro in the …'

'Yes, yes. Never mind now, Lieutenant. You can sing. Good chap.'

Allen walked over to the troops in the centre of the large square, the drum in one hand.

'What's going on?' said Carmichael.

'The officers of these men surrendered, Sir. Major Allen wants them back in military discipline and on their way before Jerry gets here.'

The three followed Allen and, when they had reached the edge of the throng, he turned to them. 'We'll start with *Tipperary*, and we'll take it from there.'

'Music hall, Sir? Our production was Mozart's …'

'The lads won't want to hear that, Lieutenant, so just sing. We'll provide accompaniment.' He brandished the drum. 'You do know the words?'

Carmichael nodded. He cleared his throat and then began making funny little gargling noises and opening and closing his mouth so wide, Harry thought the top of his head would fall off. A couple of the less inebriated soldiers watched Carmichael with growing interest. They nudged their mates, pointed and then laughter followed.

'What on earth are you doing, Lieutenant?'

Carmichael stopped, his mouth wide. 'Warming up, Sir.'

'Just get on with it, man.'

'Sir.'

Carmichael cleared his throat, looked out across his audience, and began.

'Up to mighty London Came an Irishman one day.
As the streets are paved with gold'

His voice wavered, and he hesitated, but one look at the major's face was enough.

'Sure, everyone was gay,
Singing songs of Piccadilly,
Strand and Leicester Square,
Till Paddy got excited,
Then he shouted to them there:
It's a long way to Tipperary,'

It was a well-chosen song as half the men in the square were from an Irish regiment. A few joined in with the chorus, and although Major Allen banged his drum quite out of time, and despite the trumpet only being able to manage three or four notes, within a few minutes, a fair number of the Irishmen in the audience were singing along.

Carmichael continued, buoyed by the enthusiasm of his audience:

'It's a long way to Tipperary,
It's a long way to go.
It's a long way to Tipperary

181

To the sweetest girl I know!
Goodbye, Piccadilly,
Farewell, Leicester Square!
It's a long, long way to Tipperary,
But my heart's right there.'

Allen began marching around the large square, his orchestra in close pursuit. Thomson blew his whistle as hard as he could, his face red with the effort. The two colonels stood watching from the corner of the square opposite the tethered horses. Their men came to their feet, and some began to follow close on the little band's heels, marching around the square.

The men in the square fell silent at the end of the first song, and Allen struggled to think of another, but Carmichael was on a roll.

'I'm 'Enery the Eighth, I am,
'Enery the Eighth I am, I am!

To say that the impromptu band took up the tune would be to exaggerate their talents, but they played loudly and with gusto.

' I got married to the widow next door,
She's been married seven times before
And every one was an 'Enery
She wouldn't have a Willie nor a Sam
I'm her eighth old man named 'Enery
'Enery the Eighth, I am!'

And the band played on, soldiers from around the square producing whistles, harmonicas, and one even tried his best with a Jew's harp. Allen took his band to the front of the hotel and they marched on the spot in time to the song as the men paraded past. He walked up to the hotel, climbed onto a mounting step beneath one of the arches, and turned to face them, beating his drum, its sound drowned out by the lungs of four hundred men.

They were silent at last, the echo of their words ringing around the enormous square, and then they all looked to Major Allen.

Thomson spotted the corporal who had challenged the major earlier, standing at the very back of the crowd. He slipped away from the others and ambled around the assembled troops. Sure enough, just next to the corporal stood the soldier who had aimed his rifle at the major.

'Well done, men. Well done. Your officers,' Major Allen pointed to the two colonels he had earlier spotted, and he waved them over, 'asked me to get you on your feet. Seems as if the Germans are quite some distance, and we've time yet to get away.'

There were murmurs from the crowd, not of discontent, but of approval.

Thomson moved quietly until he stood just inches behind the man who had threatened his officer. Glancing back, Thomson knew no one would see him.

'We must go now, and we must keep going,' said Allen. The two colonels took their place either side of the major. 'I won't say it will be easy, but when we're ready, we'll turn and give Jerry another bloody nose.'

There was a roar from the crowd. Thomson brought back his arm and bunched his fist.

'Just as you did at Mons.'

Another roar.

'And at Le Cateau.' Allen was having to shout to be heard, now. He waited until they settled again, and then he spoke once more. 'You are the best trained army in the world, and you have held an army of three times your own numbers at bay. Go now, and march with your heads held high. And when we're ready, we'll give Jerry a damn good hiding.'

The crowd went mad. They wanted to get hold of the Germans now. Thomson drove his arm forwards, his fist striking the soldier in the back of his neck like a train. The man dropped silently to the cobbles. And then Thomson walked back to the hotel, clapping and shouting with the rest of them.

Allen jumped off the step and spoke with the battalion commanders. 'I have not forgotten what you did this day,' he said, patting his tunic pocket. 'Now go and try to redeem yourselves.'

The colonels walked to the head of their battalions and began to march south, continuing the retreat. A small group of men remained where they had been standing. Thomson walked over. 'Alright, Corporal?'

'My mate won't get up.'

Thomson knelt next to the unconscious man. 'Hmm. Sun stroke, I should think. Leave him with us, Corporal. We'll get him onto one of the horses and see him safe home.' Thomson nodded as if he meant every word.

The corporal smiled. 'Thanks,' he said, and he and his companions ran after the departing column of infantry. Thomson dragged the unconscious soldier towards the hotel arches.

Major Allen watched the infantry go, the sound of their singing carrying clear across the square long after they'd disappeared. 'Right. Let's get after them,' he said, walking across to the three horses. 'We'll walk them for a while. Don't want to catch the infantry up and usurp the authority of their officers.'

'How did you get on with the transport, Lieutenant?' said Harry, untying his grey mare.

'There are no trains. They've all moved on. I'm afraid you're stuck with me for a bit, yet.'

'I'm getting used to this close RFC support, Sir.'

And so the four walked out of the square, leaving only a few of the braver locals staring after them across a square littered with empty wine bottles, cigarette ends, spare socks, the occasional greatcoat and various other bits of unwanted kit.

And underneath the arches of the Hotel de Ville, a toy drum, a penny whistle, a tin trumpet and an unconscious British soldier.

Sixteen

'It takes so long to get anywhere,' said Thomson.

'The roads aren't wide enough to take this volume of traffic,' said Allen.

'Up ahead, Sir,' said Harry, his sharp eyes seeing the horsemen even from a mile or so away.

Allen shielded his eyes against the late afternoon sun. 'Looks like we've finally caught up with the Cavalry Division.'

When at last they reached the distant horsemen, another couple of hours had passed. 'There must be a hundred horses here,' said Harry, suddenly feeling less afraid than he had since they had become separated back at the sugar factory.

'Yes. Bit of a mish-mash. There are men here from half a dozen cavalry regiments.' Allen looked around. 'Can't see any of ours, though.'

The horses were picketed in the field opposite an inn. Laughter carried across towards them, and turning, Allen could see officers sitting in the shade of a large chestnut tree. They appeared to be eating. His own stomach grumbled at the thought of food. 'I think this might be a suitable place to stop,' he said.

'I'll see to the horses, Sir,' said Harry, taking the head rope of the percheron.

'Good man, Thatcher. When you've dealt with them, come over.'

Harry could see that it was only officers sitting outside the inn. 'Yes, Sir,' he said, knowing he would not.

Carmichael looked across to the inn, but hesitated. He felt he would rather stay with his two companions, but they were enlisted men. 'I'm going to see if I can find out where my lot are.'

'Yes, Sir.' Harry watched Carmichael walk towards the inn. The major had already found himself a chair, and signalled for Carmichael to join them. But Carmichael held up a hand and walked past the group of dining officers. Harry watched him cross to each table and talk to the seated men. They would shake their heads, and he would walk on to the next table.

It was then that he saw the girl. She was walking towards the major's table carrying a plate in one hand and a large earthenware jug in the other. Setting them down, she turned and brushed a strand of her dark hair that had fallen across her face. She happened to look across towards the new arrivals and her eyes met Harry's. She smiled at him, and then she was gone back inside.

'Come on, Thatcher.'

Harry nodded, but didn't move, staring at the door of the inn as if it were the gateway to some magical place; and perhaps it was?

'Come on!'

Forcing himself, Harry turned to follow Thomson to the field where the cavalry horses were picketed. In typical military fashion, the horses were lined up as if for a parade. Harry secured the two mares at the end of a line using the picket post and chain that was part of the standard cavalry horse kit. He had nothing with which to secure the percheron, and so he tied its head rope to the saddle of his grey. He'd sort something better later.

Thomson had scrounged some forage from the transport limbers of another regiment, and he carried three large nets of hay over. He emptied the contents into a pile in front of each of the horses. 'There's water, too, Thatcher,' he said, pointing to a line of cavalrymen in their shirt sleeves, each carrying two canvas buckets to or from a distant stream that flowed through a copse of oaks.

'Right.' Harry unfastened the water buckets from their own horses and crossed the field. For the first time in almost a week, he didn't trouble to look over his shoulder as he walked. Instead, he thought about the girl.

*

'What the hell is that?'

The voice was instantly recognisable, and Harry's heart sank. Of all the people in the regiment to turn up, it had to be him.

'Well?' Corporal Pike stood over Harry, casting a long shadow in the last of the evening sunshine.

'It's a percheron, Corporal,' said Thomson, emerging from a dreamless sleep in an instant in the kind of way that marked out the soldier from the ordinary man. He stood and walked around the rear of the large farm horse. 'We found it in Saint-How's your father up the road.'

'Well, get rid of it before the Major sees it.'

'It's the Major's horse, Corporal.'

Pike blinked. 'Then get some tack organised for the Major, you useless pair. Unless you think he's going to want to ride bareback all the way to Paris.'

'We going to Paris, then, Corporal?' said Harry, wondering where on earth they might find spare kit.

'When the army decides what it's doing, I daresay they'll be in touch with you, Trooper Thatcher. I might ask just where you two have been for the last four days?'

'We got separated from the squadron at the sugar factory after the charge, Corporal,' said Thomson. 'Since then, we've been trying to get back.'

'You look a disgrace. And where the hell is your cap, boy?'

Harry opened his mouth to explain, and the sudden memory of the old woman's violent death stopped him from speaking.

'Well?'

'He lost it in action, Corporal.'

Pike stared at Harry and then turned away. 'Get yourselves sorted and get Major Allen some gear.'

The two watched him go, stalking across the field and no doubt looking to blight someone else's evening, thought Harry. 'It's amazing,' said Thomson at last. 'Lieutenant Smith, a decent man, gets killed, and a slug like Pike manages to come through the shambles of that charge unscathed.'

'Where are we going to find some kit for the Major's horse?'

'You leave that to me. You'd be surprised how much gear can go astray after dark.'

Harry grinned at him. 'I will leave it to you, then.' After a moment, he added: 'I wonder if anyone else is here? There must be over two hundred horses here by the looks of things. Did you see either Riley or Hardcastle? At the sugar factory, I mean?'

Thomson didn't answer.

'What happened to them, Thomson?'

'I don't know about Riley, but Hardcastle was hit by a shell. Right in front of me. Blown to tatters, he was.'

'But Riley might be alright?'

'Maybe.'

Neither spoke for a while.

'I'm going to see if I can get some more grub,' said Thomson at length. 'After the last four days, I don't want to have to go hungry again if I can help it.'

'I'll go and report to the Major.'

Harry walked to a gap in the hedgerow and passed through it. He crossed the rough track that ran past the edge of the field and then the road that led north to Saint-Quentin and south to who knew where?

'Ah, Thatcher.' It was Carmichael. Harry had almost forgotten the RFC lieutenant during the afternoon, so delighted was he to have been returned to the bosom of at least a part of the Brigade.

'Sir.'

Carmichael returned his salute. 'I've managed to find out where my lot are. Or were, at least. I've got myself a ride first thing in the morning in motorised transport. No more horses for me.'

'I'm pleased, Sir. It's good to be back amongst your own.'

'I wanted to thank you; in case I don't see you or Trooper Thomson in the morning. I wouldn't have come this far without you, that's certain.'

'We made a good team, Sir. You and that lethal weapon.'

'Yes. That's a thought. I should like that shotgun back.'

Harry turned and pointed back across the lane and into the field. 'That's us on the end of the line, Sir. I should think we'll be pressing on at dawn, too. Thomson will have your gun somewhere, Sir.'

'Right. I shall come over and see you before I leave.'

'I thought I should report to the Major. Haven't seen him for an hour or so.'

'I think he was inside earlier, Thatcher. Try there.'

Harry saluted again and headed for the inn. Standing at the door, he could hear music. Someone had got a gramophone and Harry listened, trying to recognise the tune. He was standing there when the girl came to the door.

'*Excusez-moi.*' She stood and waited for him to respond. He just looked at her. Her eyes were brown. He tried to think of a suitable comparison, and his mind alighted on the horse chestnuts of autumn; the tree in the school yard. He tried to brush the thought away; she did not have eyes like conkers.

'Both times I have seen you, you have stared at me,' she continued in French.

And her skin, so tanned.

'Are you alright?' she said, smiling now.

'Her teeth are so white,' he said after a lengthy pause.

'Pardon?'

'What?'

'My teeth are so white? You said my teeth are white.'

He'd no idea he had spoken aloud. He felt his face burning with embarrassment. 'I meant …' but he could add nothing that didn't make him appear more stupid.

'Your French is very good,' she said, taking pity on him. 'The English officers all speak French, but they make it sound incomprehensible. You have a good accent.'

'Can I help you with that?' He noticed that she was carrying a heap of dirty plates and cutlery and was keen to change the subject.

'Yes, if you like. Why don't you take these through to the kitchen. I'll get the rest.'

He held out his hands and she placed the crockery in them, the knives and forks on top. 'At the back.' She pointed through the door.

He nodded and walked through. Officers from every cavalry regiment in the Division sat about inside the inn, drinking coffee or brandy, smoking their pipes and sharing stories of their various exploits in the great retreat. Harry saw Major Allen at the back of the room. He was studying a gramophone disc, holding it to the fading light from a window to read the label. Apparently satisfied, he placed the disc onto the turntable and began to wind the handle.

'Sir.'

'Ah, Thatcher.' Allen turned at Harry's voice. 'I see you're keeping yourself busy, lad. Well done. And no wonder,' he added, looking across to the door. 'She's very pretty. If I was ten years younger, I am sure I should be clearing the tables, too.' He smiled.

'More like twenty,' shouted a captain from a nearby table, obviously somewhat the worse for wear after an afternoon spent in the convivial company of fellow officers, and cavalrymen to boot.

Allen frowned, and then he smiled at Harry again. 'We're off at first light, Thatcher, so get some rest, and bring the horses over before it gets light.'

'Thomson said he'd find you some tack, Sir.'

'I know that Trooper Thomson is a very resourceful man, so I don't doubt it. I just pity the fellow who has to ride without a saddle tomorrow.'

The girl walked past the two of them. Allen lowered the arm onto the disc. A crackle filled the room as the needle sought the groove. 'On your way, Trooper,' said Allen.

'Yes, Sir.' Seeing no way to salute, Harry nodded his head in what he hoped was a formal manner, and then followed the girl into the kitchen.

The back door of the inn had been thrown open to allow some air through into the suffocating heat of the kitchen. One man worked at the stove, a huge heap of eggshells to his left. Harry watched as he broke another three into a pan sizzling with what smelled like butter. He used only one hand to crack and open the egg before adding the halves of shell to the pile.

A younger man stood at a sink and worked a cloth across the face of a plate before dipping it into the water and then stacking it to one side. The pile of dirty crockery would have been enough to weaken most men's resolve, but he worked on.

The girl placed her own collection of plates onto the dirty pile and motioned for Harry to do the same.

'Who is this?' said the cook, turning to look across at Harry, all the while moving the omelette in the pan.

'He is a British cavalryman, papa,' she said.

'Man? He's a boy. I doubt he even shaves.'

Harry rubbed his chin, sure he could feel a few days' stubble.

'Why don't you ask him, papa? He speaks very good French.'

The girl's father grunted something. He was suspicious of young men of his daughter's age. He knew she was beautiful, and he knew how young men were around beautiful girls. Knew what they wanted. It was what he had wanted as a boy. He grunted again and reached for the salt cellar. He took a generous pinch, sprinkled it between his finger tips and then upended the omelette onto a plate. 'Here.' He held it out to the girl, but stared into Harry's eyes.

She took the plate, and Harry followed her out of the back door.

'Don't mind him,' she said.

'No.'

'He's a bit over-protective. Since mother died.' She put the plate down in front of a young lieutenant. He stood at her arrival, made to introduce himself, but she had already left. He sat back down, stared after her for a moment, and then took up his fork, watching Harry with envy.

'I'm sorry,' said Harry. 'About your mother.'

She shrugged. 'I didn't know her. But it's still a terrible thing to lose a parent, isn't it?'

Harry didn't respond. Some parents weren't worth the keeping.

'You can help me, if you want?'

'Yes, I'd like that.'

'What's your name?' she said, turning to face him at the kitchen door.

'Harry. Harry Thatcher.'

'*Arreee. Arreee Satcher.*'

He smiled. 'Huh. Huh. Harry.'

She tried again, but not much better. She laughed, and again he felt his stomach lurch. Like the first time he had to jump Lucy in the exercise paddock. No, different. A nice fear.

She waited, but when he failed to ask her name, she sighed. She was used to the effect she had on men, barely noticed it now. It had started a few years earlier, and at first she had not understood why they gaped; why their wives gave her such icy, contemptuous stares.

'I am Geneviève.'

They continued to look at one another.

'There is food waiting to be served in here,' said her father from the kitchen. 'When you have finished gawping at each other.'

'Yes, papa.'

They went through laughing, and Geneviève's father glared at Harry. He took the proffered plate, and then the two of them went back outside into the comparative cool of the evening to serve up the omelettes.

They soon got into a routine. Harry would take the orders, in English, from the men sitting in and around the inn, and then Geneviève would take them through to her father, and then the two of them would serve the food and wine to the clientele.

They didn't speak much, but it seemed as if there was no need. They smiled as they passed one another to and from the kitchen, and Harry loved the feeling that all the men of the Brigade were watching the girl; the girl with whom he was spending the evening.

They could have gone on all night, serving food to men who seemed to have an endless appetite for omelettes, which was the only thing on offer, and cheap, local red wine. But the supply of eggs was finite, and Geneviève's father announced that he was cooking the last two. Harry and Geneviève stood in the kitchen, the boy still washing the dishes, in ignorance of the light dying outside.

'Here,' said her father. 'For the two of you. You must be hungry.'

'Thank you, Sir,' said Harry, taking the plates.

Her father looked at him while he retrieved a part smoked cigarette from behind his ear, presumably stored there when the horses of the British cavalry had begun to arrive in the late afternoon. Taking a match, he struck it against the rough wood of a kitchen cupboard. He inhaled and then grunted in the way Harry had learned that Frenchmen do. It seemed to express disdain, disappointment, acceptance, warning even, in a single sound.

Geneviève laughed. 'Don't look so fierce, papa. You'll frighten him.' She took Harry's arm, grabbed two forks from the drainer, and then they left by the back door.

Her father watched the night swallow them up and then turned to his son. 'You keep an eye on them, Marcel.'

'Yes, father,' said the boy, who had no intention of doing any such thing.

'Hmm.'

*

Harry tried his best to hold back, but he was starving. He had cleared his plate before she'd had time to eat even a half of her omelette.

'Here, you have the rest of mine.'

'No, I'm fine,' said Harry, staring at her plate.

'Go, on, *Arreee*. You are hungry.'

He smiled, and then he swapped their plates, and her supper was soon gone. He stood to return the plates to the kitchen.

'No,' she said. 'My father will only find something else for us to do. Leave them. Let's go for a walk.'

She took his hand, and he heard his heart beat in his own ears.

'Why did you become a soldier?' They were walking along the stream bank, away from the inn and the field where the horses were picketed.

'I don't know. My brother? He's in the army, and it seemed like a good idea at the time.'

'I have seen the men of the village march away,' she said. 'My father says he will go, but I think, I hope, he is too old. Marcel will go. I think it will be bad.'

Harry nodded. 'It is,' he said, and thought of the farmer's wife again. 'But they say it will be over by Christmas,' he added, trying to lighten the mood.

'Perhaps.'

They walked on a bit further to where the stream came down a hillside. She led him up the hill a little way to where an old oak stood. She leaned back against the rough trunk, and he did the same.

He could see the inn's lights burning about a half mile away across the fields. The music from the gramophone and the men's laughter carried faintly across to them. It was hard to believe that there was a war; that they were being hunted down by a German army of over twice their number.

He was very aware of her presence: the rustle of her skirts, the press of her arm against his. She turned to him. 'I'm afraid. Hold me, *Arreee*.'

He turned awkwardly, suddenly self-conscious. She sensed his uncertainty. 'Do you want to kiss me, *Arreee*?' she said, so softly that he almost didn't hear her. She tilted her head back a little, parted her lips, and he leaned in, pressed his mouth to hers in a clumsy movement, but she was ready. And then he forgot his awkwardness.

Much later, they walked back towards the inn. The music had gone, exhaustion overcoming the officers' enthusiasm to party. They picked their way carefully between sleeping bodies and at the door to the inn, he kissed her goodnight; a long, lingering kiss, and she drew back, her hands still at his waist. 'My. You soldiers are all the same!' She smiled, and with that, she was gone.

Harry stood at the door for a moment longer and then, grinning to himself, he walked back across the road and squeezed through the gap in the hedge. He made his way along the line of picketed horses until he found his own. He curled up on the ground a few yards from Thomson's sleeping form, and within moments, he fell asleep, still wearing a big grin.

Seventeen

'Time to say goodbye, chaps. I've got some transport back to my squadron.'

'Good luck, Sir.' Thomson stuck out his hand without thinking.

Carmichael smiled, taking the Trooper's hand. 'And to you, Thomson. I don't think we could have managed without you.'

'Goodbye, Sir,' said Harry, suddenly concerned that they would be without the Lieutenant's guidance. The three shared a look.

'You'd better be on your way,' said Carmichael.

Thomson nodded, and the two turned to their horses.

'Oh, Thomson. Do you have my shotgun?'

Thomson reached into the rifle bucket on the bay mare and withdrew the weapon.

'What the hell is that?'

'When we were in town, I took the liberty of shortening it, Sir.'

Carmichael took the gun and turned it over in his hands.

'I sawed the top two feet of barrel off, Sir, and a bit of the stock.'

'I can see that, but why, man? Why?'

'I don't know much about flying, Sir, but I don't suppose you've a lot of room up there, and this still works with the bits sawn off. You'll have a bit more space to swing it around, Sir.'

Carmichael thought about it. He could see Thomson was right. 'Well, thank you, Thomson. I appreciate it.'

'You could probably fashion a holster for it so you could carry it on your belt, Sir.'

'Yes, I think the squadron commander might have something to say about that, but thank you all the same.'

'Welcome, Sir.'

'Do you want your pistol back, Sir?'

'No, Thatcher. You keep it. I'll get another.'

The three looked at one another again. A toot from the road interrupted the silence, and Carmichael turned at the sound. 'My ride,' he said, seeing the motor lorry. 'Good luck, boys.'

They watched him cross the road, step up into the vehicle, and then while the driver crunched the gears, they watched the lorry pull away in a cloud of dust and exhaust smoke.

'And don't forget, I owe you a trip in a plane, young Thatcher,' said Carmichael, shouting from an open window of the lorry, and then he was gone.

'Come on. Best get these horses over to the Major before someone spots they don't have a saddle.'

'Where did you get it?' Harry admired the polished tack on the back of the percheron. It gleamed as if its erstwhile owner had spent a lifetime working on the leather, bringing it up to perfection.

'Don't ask.'

A shout came from further along the picket line.

'Come on, Thatcher, let's go. Quick.'

They led the horses over the road and stood in the area between the tables and chairs outside the inn. Major Allen walked towards them, running a comb through his hair. He slipped it into his tunic pocket and replaced his cap on his head.

'Well done, Thomson. I knew you'd find something. Do we have time for a *café-au-lait*?' Allen looked past the horses across the lane to where a corporal was running up and down the line of horses, shouting at anyone and everyone. 'Or is the theft discovered already?'

'We should probably leave right now, Sir.'

'Right you are.' With that, the three mounted and Allen and Thomson began to move off. Harry held back, staring across at the inn.

'Come on, Thatcher,' said Thomson, stopping to look back.

He saw her in an upstairs window. She waved down to him, and then disappeared.

'Get a move on, lads,' came Allen's voice from along the road.

'Yes, Sir,' said Thomson. 'Harry?'

The girl ran from the door of the inn and across to Harry. He swung his leg out over the grey's head and slipped down from the saddle. He took her in his arms and kissed her.

Major Allen had stopped a little way on, turning ready to shout at what remained of his squadron, but his words stopped in his throat. He smiled. A minute passed, and Thomson was sure that either Thatcher or the girl would have to draw back for breath.

'I must go,' Harry said at last, holding her at arms' length. 'I won't forget you, Geneviève. Ever.'

'After last night, I should hope not, *Arreee Satcher*.'

'I think I love you,' he said, and for some reason he could not fathom, tears sprang to his eyes.

'Perhaps. Now go.'

He nodded, cuffed at his tears, and with one look back, he swung up into the saddle.

'*Good luck, Arreee Satcher*,' she said in English.

He dug his heels into the horse. The mare, half asleep, lifted her head suddenly and then began to walk forwards. Harry drew level with Thomson.

He smiled across at Harry. 'So that's how it is, you sly dog. I wondered where you were last night. I'd say you were the envy of every man in this rag tag regiment.'

The three of them made their way onto the road. They had almost rounded the bend when a shout came from behind them. 'Wait!' Corporal Pike trotted along, bouncing uncomfortably on the bare back of his horse. 'I'll have you for this, Thomson, you beggar!'

'You didn't?' said Harry, staring across at Thomson.

Thomson grinned, and Pike bounced past the two of them, holding a dirty piece of rope that went around his horse's neck, determined to catch up with Major Allen. 'Sir!'

'Yes, Corporal Pike?'

'It seems like Thomson's stolen my kit, Sir. Put it on your horse, Sir.'

'I don't think so, Corporal. This is my gear.'

Pike stopped in the road, unable to think of anything to say to that flat denial.

'Come on, boys. We've a long way to go until we catch up with the rest of the Regiment. Wherever they are.'

Harry and Thomson passed Pike as he sat motionless on his horse. They kept their eyes forward, and eventually he kicked on his gelding and brought up the rear of their party.

Harry looked back towards the inn only once more, but it had passed beyond the bend. He wondered if he would ever see the girl with the conker-brown eyes again.

*

The road was littered with the flotsam and jetsam of war: overturned carts, occasional bits of clothing, here and there a dead animal, and curiously, some larger pieces of furniture. Harry stared at the leather topped oak desk as he passed, and he tried to imagine why it would be so important to its owner that they would carry it along this road with an enemy army in pursuit.

There were fewer civilians on the road now. Perhaps they thought that this far into France, they'd be safe from the Germans? But Harry knew that was a false hope. They would never be safe.

It was getting hot again, and Harry regretted the loss of his cap, and that brought the memory of the farm once more. He wondered if he would ever forget that, and then he wondered if he should even try. Perhaps it was right that he always remember the old woman?

As they passed, a cloud of flies lifted from the corpse of a dog. Harry looked away. In the distance, he could make out a line of horses and as he studied them more closely, he realised they were horse drawn artillery. 'Sir?'

'Yes, Thatcher.'

'To our left, Sir; a battery of artillery.'

'Theirs or ours?'

'Hard to say, Sir, at this distance.'

Allen cursed the loss of his horse in the fighting at Le Cateau. It had been shot from under him, and with it had gone all his kit, including his beautiful Zeiss field glasses. But he had to know who they were. 'Do you feel like taking a little canter over yonder and finding out, Thatcher?'

'Yes, Sir.'

'Good man. We'll wait off the road here.'

Harry took his rifle from the bucket and checked it was loaded. He knew it ought to be; he'd barely fired it. Slotting it back, he glanced down on the left to be sure of his sword, although what difference his pathetic armaments would be against the two hundred strong artillery battery, he didn't know. He dug his heels into the grey, and she responded.

Thomson watched the lad go, a concerned look on his face.

'I just hope if he gets himself killed, the horse comes back so I can get the saddle.' It was Pike, and Thomson felt his jaw muscles tighten.

Harry felt the familiar fear at the impending action but, for the first time, he felt able to manage it; to push it back so he could get on with what he'd been asked to do. He kept his eyes on the distant horsemen and aimed for a point ahead of them where they would intersect. He guessed that by now, he would be visible to the more sharp-eyed amongst the battery.

He couldn't tell a British artillery piece from a German one from a mile away. He urged his horse to a gallop, keen to close the distance; to get it over with. And then he knew who they were by the colour of their uniforms: khaki green; they were British. He just hoped they knew he was, too.

Interested faces looked across as he came at them from the side, racing along the line of horses and guns. He came to the front where he assumed he would find the officers and reined in ahead of them. 'Who are you, Sir?' he said, spotting a major in the front rank.

'Major Robertshaw, L Battery, Royal Horse Artillery. And you, young man?'

'L Battery, Sir?'

'Yes.'

'I'm Trooper Thatcher, Sir.'

The major turned to his left. 'We've a Thatcher in the battery, haven't we, Captain Dawe?'

The captain opened his mouth to reply, but Harry spoke first: 'I know, Sir,' he said. 'He's my brother!'

*

'We're joining the rest of the 1st Cavalry Brigade, Major Allen,' said Robertshaw. The two rode side by side, the rest of the battery strung out behind them. 'They'll be a few miles ahead, I expect.'

Allen nodded. 'We got separated from the 2nd Cavalry Brigade some days ago. Been trying to catch up since.'

'We had some of your chaps with us earlier in the week, Allen. After the action at that village south of the forest at Mormal. They've gone their own way, now. But you're welcome to join us, if you wish? Until you find your own way home. And I'm sure we can find you a better mount.' Robertshaw looked at Allen's liberated carthorse, quite unimpressed.

Allen smiled. 'He's a stout fellow,' he said, slapping the percheron's thick neck, 'but perhaps if you've something a little more lively, I should be grateful. And some tack for my corporal?'

'See to it, Captain,' said Robertshaw. Captain Dawe, riding just behind the two majors, turned and headed back down towards the rear of the column in search of the quartermaster sergeant.

'We could do with your lad, too.'

'Thatcher?'

'Yes. We could put him with his brother in Lieutenant Wright's section; Wright's bugler was killed at Mons.'

'I'm sure he'd appreciate that.'

'And we could use your other men at Regimental HQ. Always handy to have a couple of extra hands.'

'By all means, Robertshaw.'

'That's settled, then.'

*

'I could get used to this,' said Harry.

'What, bully beef and army biscuit?'

'No, Richard. It's just nice to be back with a full regiment, even if it's not ours.'

'And after a week on the run without any food to speak of, even this is good,' said Thomson. 'Although hard on the teeth,' he added, lifting his right hand to his lower jaw.

The others laughed.

'So how have you been getting along, little brother?'

Harry glanced at Thomson. There was so much to say. 'Alright,' he said, shrugging. 'I can see you've done well, Richard. Promoted?'

Richard grinned. 'I was, Harry. I'm the leader, now. Bombardier Thatcher, at your service. Malone and Dovey here,' he indicated the others of his sub-section, 'have to do what I say. Isn't that right, lads?'

'If you say so, Bomb,' said Malone, chasing the last scrap of beef around his mess tin with his spoon.

'So, how have you been, Harry?'

'I've been fine, Richard.'

'I saw your lot go in, charging the guns.'

'We were there. Thomson and me.'

'The charge just fell apart. What happened?'

'Barbed wire across the field. Couldn't see it,' said Thomson.

'Where are we going, Bombardier?' said Harry, smiling across at his brother.

'They don't keep us too well informed. We're in constant action, racing from one place to another to engage Jerry, holding them back, and then leaving just when the fight gets going.'

'This your brother, Bombardier?'

Harry and Richard turned at the voice. Harry made to stand up.

'As you were, lads,' said the young officer standing behind them.

'Yes, Sir. This is Harry, Sir.'

'Delighted to meet another member of the Thatcher family.'

'Thank you, Sir.'

'Lieutenant Wright is the officer commanding our section, Harry. A section is two guns, ours, F gun, and that shambles in E gun over there.' Richard pointed to another gun and its crew.

'Nice mount, Thatcher,' said Wright, walking along the line of tethered horses that stood next to the gun and its ammunition limber.

'Not mine, Sir.'

'Oh?'

'We found her wandering in the woods south of Mons.'

'I'll bet someone's sorry they lost her. Fine animal.' Wright ran his hands up and down the grey's legs, feeling the muscle tone. 'Very fine. Well, carry on, lads.'

Richard watched him cross to the other gun crew. Within moments, there was laughter.

'We're a good team, Harry. We've got good officers.'

The thought of Lieutenant Smith, his hand still clutching his beautiful sword, crossed Harry's mind, but he pushed the image away. 'Yes, that's important,' he said.

'Right,' said Richard. 'I think we should try to get some kip. Major Robertshaw wants us off at dawn, which means getting the guns hooked up an hour before. I got you a blanket each, so get your heads down. We'll probably find the rest of the Brigade tomorrow.'

*

With little to do, Harry wandered along the horse lines. He sniffed. There was something deeply comforting about the smell: an amalgam of horse sweat, leather tack, forage and even manure, he thought to himself, looking down at his boots; the smell of a cavalry regiment on the move.

Men stood with their shirts off, their braces hanging at their knees, as they washed and shaved in small cups of water, or the dregs of their tea. And then the camp was struck: kit loaded onto the limbers; blankets and groundsheets rolled and fixed to saddles.

Then Harry watched the men as they manoeuvred the horses that would haul the guns all day. Watched while they ensured that the harnesses and straps were comfortable but correctly tightened. Officers and NCOs moved among the men, but the men knew what they were doing and needed little guidance.

Draining the remains of his tea, long cold, Harry pushed his borrowed mess tin back into his pack. The mare turned her head to watch him as he swung up into the saddle. She blew through her nose and then dragged a front hoof through the dust of the forest floor, perhaps signalling her desire to get moving. Harry felt it, too. The need to get going.

He hadn't long to wait. They were back on the road by five, Harry riding next to Lieutenant Wright at the rear of the two guns that made up his section. They cleared the forest of Compiegne where they had spent the night, and the sunshine, already warm, was welcome.

'What's the river, Sir?'

'I think that's the Aisne, Thatcher. Joins to the Seine in Paris.'

'We going to Paris, Sir?'

Wright shook his head. 'I shouldn't think so. Just keeping one step ahead of the Germans. They're probably headed for Paris, though, so who knows?'

Harry felt proud as he watched his brother lead F gun across the river at a narrow, arched bridge somewhere between Soissons and Compiegne.

Wright looked across and smiled. 'He's good, your brother. First class artilleryman, and brilliant on a horse. Did you do much riding when you were young?'

Harry laughed. 'No, Sir. Neither of us had ever seen a horse before we joined up.'

'Well, that just proves that some men are natural born horsemen.'

Corporal Pike, like Thomson, now attached to Regimental HQ, crashed across the bridge like a bull in a china shop.

'And others less so,' said Wright. He nodded at engineers that stood at the side of the road waiting for the battery to pass. 'They'll blow the bridge when we're across. Hopefully delay the Germans.'

Harry looked back and, sure enough, the engineers were already laying charges beneath the solid Roman arches of the old bridge. The two of them trotted up the far bank. Paris was now only fifty miles to the southwest.

*

Richard reined in, bringing the team to a stop. Eight o'clock in the evening, and the rest of the Brigade were here already, he noticed. But it had probably been wise to water the horses back at the last town, even if it meant arriving late.

He looked right and left, and satisfied that his own gun was in line with the rest, he swung down from his horse and stretched his back. He and the rest of the gun's crew began to unhitch the three pairs of horses that pulled gun and its limber. Rynd and Moore, two of the seventeen men that crewed the gun, took the horses and led them out of the way. Everyone had a job, and they all knew how to do theirs.

Within a few minutes, the entire battery was lined up east to west in a field just south of the small hamlet of Néry. The horses of the battery were tethered between the guns in neat lines. It was the first time in a week that Major Robertshaw had felt secure enough to order the guns to be unhitched.

Richard wiped the sweat from his forehead, and looked towards the hamlet where most of the rest of the Brigade was billeted. He glanced to the west, and saw the lines of the Queen's Bays in the field on the other side of the road.

'I'm going to report to Brigade, Lieutenant Wright. You carry on here,' said Major Robertshaw, watching the F gun crew.

'We'll join you if we may, Sir?' said Major Allen, indicating Pike, Thomson and Harry.

'Of course. Keen to find your regiment, eh? Come on, then.'

The five of them trotted out of the field and along the road that ran north-south between the sugar factory and the hamlet to the north. They found Brigade HQ in the Mairie on the west side of the road.

'Secure the horses,' said Allen, walking after Robertshaw.

Harry and Thomson began to fasten the horses by their head ropes to a railing that ran around the front garden of the stone building.

Pike lit a cigarette and watched the others. He was still furious about the loss of his saddle, and despite having it back now, he was looking for an opportunity to sort Thomson. He turned as Allen came back out of the house.

'Could you come in, Thatcher?' he said before disappearing back inside.

Harry looked at Thomson who shrugged. He walked up the short path that led into the house. Stepping inside, Harry looked around, and then hearing voices, he made his way to the back of the building.

A door opened onto a large kitchen, and as Harry stepped through, Major Allen turned at the sound of his boots on the flagstones of the hall. 'Ah, here he is, Sir,' said Allen, motioning Harry forwards.

Harry walked into the kitchen, and a dozen faces turned to look at the young newcomer; the faces of some senior officers. He stood next to Major Allen and saluted the most senior man in the room.

'I understand you've had some adventures, young man?'

'Yes, Sir.'

'Well, I'm going to borrow you, if I may. We need a few messengers here at Brigade, and your major's volunteered you and your colleague. Alright?'

Harry nodded at the tall, silver-haired officer.

'Carry on then, Major.'

Allen and Harry both saluted and then turned on their heels.

'Just stay where I can find you, Trooper,' came the officer's voice from the kitchen.

Harry turned and stepped back through into the kitchen. 'Yes, Sir.' And then he joined Major Allen back in the hall. 'Who was that, Sir?'

'Brigadier-General Briggs. He commands this brigade, Thatcher.'

Harry frowned.

'I think you're very lucky,' said Allen, knowing that Harry probably wanted to be with his brother. 'You'll doubtless spend a quiet night here in the Mayor's house, feet up and sipping coffee.'

Harry nodded, but he was disappointed.

'You'll have Thomson for company.'

'Yes, Sir.' Harry brightened; he hadn't been sure to whom the brigadier had referred when he'd said 'your colleague'. It could have been Pike.

'Right. I'm off, then. Corporal Pike and I are to ride to Division; find out where the rest of our own brigade is.' He smiled, returned Harry's salute, and was gone.

Harry looked around. There was a small armchair in the corner of the hall by the stairs. He walked over and sat down on the edge of the seat. After a few minutes, no one had come asking him to deliver any messages, and so he edged his buttocks further back. He wondered where Thomson was, but assumed Major Allen had found him something to do. Then he leaned back, closed his eyes for just a moment, and was asleep in seconds.

*

Unknown to the men of the British 1st Cavalry Brigade, over five thousand men and horses of the German 4th Cavalry Division crossed the River Oise to their north, using a Roman bridge that had managed to withstand the best efforts of the British engineers to destroy it. They rode on through the late evening, searching for the British cavalry screen that they knew was ahead. As darkness fell, they looked for somewhere to billet for the night.

Eighteen

'Thatcher.'

Harry could hear a voice, but he ignored it.

'Thatcher.'

The speaker shook his leg, and Harry blinked. 'Thomson?'

'Come on. The Brigadier wants us to go with a couple of Hussars on a patrol across the ravine.'

'Ravine?' said Harry, still not sure where he was.

'Other side of the village, the hills to the east. I was in the kitchen helping myself to coffee, and Brigadier Briggs said he wanted someone from Brigade to go with the Hussars, but then he remembered us. Come on.'

Harry pushed himself from the chair where he'd spent the last couple of hours and groaned. 'I'm stiff as a post.'

'See; you've got used to sleeping on the ground.'

They stepped outside. Two Hussars, an officer and a corporal, waited already mounted up the road a little. They looked around as Thomson and Harry appeared from the Mairie.

Harry pulled himself onto the back of his horse. 'I can hardly see beyond those two.'

'It's fog,' said Thomson. 'Came down last night around midnight while you were sleeping like a baby in your comfy armchair.'

Harry felt the water soak through his trousers from the damp on the saddle. 'What are we looking for?'

'Probably nothing. Just having a quick scout around the outskirts of the village before we set off,' said Thomson, his rifle across his lap as he checked it was loaded. He slotted it back into its bucket on his right.

'Alright, chaps?' said the officer. 'Lieutenant Taylor,' he added by way of introduction.

'Sir.'

He said nothing further, and the four made their way north along the road out of the village. A crossroads came into view through the swirling fog no more than ten yards distant. The lieutenant stopped and looked both ways before urging his horse to the right. Shortly after, the road forked. The party took the path to the left, passing a group of soldiers guarding the road. Leaving the small village behind, they climbed the gentle slope of the hill that led up into the woods, still invisible through the mist.

They splashed through a stream and then Harry began to feel the hill getting steeper beneath their feet. Taylor led them in a zig-zag course, following a track worn in the hillside by sheep over decades of use.

The path was narrow and they fell into single file, with Harry at the rear. Harry was panting when they reached the plateau, and his mare was blowing hard after the climb, the air ahead of Harry swirling with the mist and her hot breath.

They rode on for a few more minutes and could still see nothing. Taylor turned to his corporal and was about to give the order to return to the village, when he heard a voice from the fog. He turned his head, angling his ear to try to hear the voice. There it was again. He looked at the others. 'Probably some scouts from one of the other regiments,' he said, scarce above a whisper.

Harry shook his head. 'No, Sir. That was German.'

Taylor raised his eyebrows. 'You sure?'

'He's fluent, Sir,' said Thomson.

Taylor turned to look northeast again. He stared into the folds of fog, willing them to part and expose the owners of the disembodied voices. 'There,' he said after a moment.

Harry looked and, sure enough, he could see horsemen. Figures so indistinct, they could be anyone. Taylor rubbed his chin. He'd been warned there were possibly French in the hills around the village, but the lad seemed sure about the language.

The shot when it came surprised not only the distant horsemen, but Taylor, Thomson and Harry. The corporal had fired his Lee Enfield at the mist-shrouded figures, and they watched a man fall from his horse. A freak movement of the air around the unknown cavalry brushed the fog aside for a brief moment, and with a heavy feeling in his stomach, Taylor knew he was looking at a squadron of German cavalry.

'Back,' he shouted, and he yanked at the bit, dragging his horse to face the other direction. A shout went up as the Germans spotted their attackers, realised how few they were, and gave chase.

Harry turned the grey to face back down the hillside, but they had moved away from the sheep run, and he couldn't find it. He dug in his heels, and headed down the hill and trusted to the mare's eyes and instincts. It was so steep that his feet were almost up by the horse's head in his efforts to stay in the saddle.

A shot rang out, muffled by the enveloping fog, and whether this was a friendly shot, or from some German carbine, he would never know. Taylor was just ahead and had found a rough track. 'Here, lads,' he shouted back, and Harry nudged the grey to his right to intersect with the path.

He could hear angry German voices behind and above them as they searched for their enemy along the ridge. The path was clearly used by more than sheep, and was wider. Taylor, keen to get to Brigade, urged his horse to a gallop, and then he was down in a flurry of limbs.

His horse came to his feet and stood a few yards further on, dazed but apparently unhurt. Taylor, badly winded, walked towards his horse, saw the rabbit hole in the path that had been his misfortune, and then while the corporal held his mount, he clambered back into the saddle, wincing as his ribs grated.

Excited shouts from behind them, and Thomson turned to face back up the track. The mist swirled again, and there were the Germans, the track discovered, and they were coming on hard. The mist swallowed them, and Thomson urged his horse off the track and into a gorse bush beneath a tree at the side. The others followed his lead, and Harry had only just cleared the track when the first German came past.

A low branch of the tree brushed the man's helmet, knocking it off his head, and the group of horsemen continued on down the hill. The four British cavalrymen waited for a minute or so longer.

'They must not have all come down,' said Taylor. 'If we head across the hillside, we can get back to the village more quickly and, with luck, avoid them.'

Harry jumped off his horse and walked into the track. He bent down and picked up the German helmet.

'Souvenir, Trooper?'

'Thought someone might be able to identify the unit from the helmet, Sir,' said Harry, swinging his leg over the saddle as he mounted.

'Good thinking. Come on, let's go.'

Taylor led them across the track and into the fog beyond. They picked their way down the hillside until they crossed another of the sheep tracks, following it to the bottom of the hill. They found themselves just outside the village.

'I'm going to report to my regiment,' said Taylor. 'Corporal, you head along the main road and find the 5th Dragoon Guards and let them know what we saw.'

The corporal nodded, and was off into the mist to find the other cavalry regiment.

'And you two get back to Brigade and let them know there are uhlans in the woods.'

Thomson and Harry found a road that led into the village and trotted along it. They were challenged by the same pickets they had passed on their way out, and then continued on to the crossroads. As they turned onto the main road heading south, Harry realised he could see the length of the road; the fog was lifting, and daylight was coming.

*

Four men stood around the kitchen table looking at the German helmet. It wasn't like the flat topped helmets Harry had seen before, but had a spike.

'Uhlans?' said Major Crawford.

Brigadier Briggs shook his head. 'Cuirassiers.' He lifted his eyes from the helmet. 'What exactly did you see, Trooper?'

'What looked like a hundred enemy horsemen, Sir. Some followed us down the hillside, but we managed to lose them.'

'Where did Taylor go?'

'He went to alert the Hussars, Sir, and sent his corporal to the 5th Dragoons up the road.'

'Good. It's probably just an advance guard and you were lucky, or unlucky, to bump into them as they scouted ahead,' said the major.

Briggs looked at his brigade major. 'Perhaps, Major, but perhaps not.'

He was about to say more when there was a crash. The four men ducked involuntarily, and a piece of the ceiling came down, lathe and plaster falling over the kitchen table.

Something landed across the floor against the kitchen range. Briggs walked over, and bending down he looked at it. 'German fuze,' he said, turning to face the others. Nobody needed to say how lucky they'd been that the shell had not gone off.

'Sound the alarm, Trooper. I think it's more than an advance guard out there in the mist,' said Briggs, and Harry turned for the door and ran down the hall to his horse. 'And you,' Briggs pointed to Thomson. 'Do you know where Verberie is?'

Thomson nodded. 'We watered the horses there last night, Sir. About five miles north.'

'The 4th Infantry Division is bivouacked there.' Briggs began scribbling a note with a pencil. 'Get this message to General Snow. I think we're going to need their help.'

Thomson took the paper and slipped it into his tunic pocket, nodded, and ran for the door.

'Where's the rest of the Cavalry Division, Major?

'Saint-Vaast, Sir.'

'Organise a couple of motorcycle riders to get a message to General Allenby there, then.'

'Yes, Sir.'

Outside, Thomson unhitched his horse, swung up into the saddle, and looked over as Harry took up his borrowed bugle. 'See you later,' he said, and with a hard kick to his horse's ribs, he galloped off up the road heading north for help that couldn't possibly arrive in time.

Harry blew into the bugle. A strangled sound came from the instrument, and he licked at his lips, and then tried again. But it wasn't necessary. More shells began to fall on the village, crashing into the buildings around Harry, and there wasn't a man in the village who didn't know they were under attack.

The major came running from the Mairie, and another shell passed through the tiled roof of the house before striking the ground near him. Harry was knocked flat by the blast, the bugle spinning off across the road. He lay on his back, staring at the sky, confused, his ears humming with a constant sound. He realised he was still alive and, moving his arms and legs, he understood that he was unhurt. He rolled onto his knees, coughed, and then looked over to the house. Blood was splashed up the brickwork, and the flagstones that led to the front door were ripped up and tossed aside as if made of paper. Of Major Crawford, there was no sign.

It was then that Harry thought about his brother. Standing up, he stumbled to the twisted remains of the wrought iron fence that surrounded the house's small front garden. He unfastened the head rope, clambered up into the saddle, and kicked his mare to a gallop down the road towards L Battery.

L Battery who were billeted in the open, plainly visible from the surrounding heights. Easy pickings for the German gunners.

Nineteen

At first light, the men of the battery were striking camp, moving on with the rest of the Brigade, ready to patrol the ground to the northwest of Paris.

Richard took another mouthful of his breakfast, slices of bacon and twice-baked bread, and took a swig from his enamel cup, a luxury he'd acquired before arriving in France. He looked to the south. The sugar factory was all but invisible in the fog that had sprung up shortly after midnight, but Richard saw Lieutenant Wright appear from that direction with Sergeant Harris.

'All ready to depart, Bombardier?'

'Yes, Sir.'

'We're going to wait until this fog clears, I think.'

Richard looked over to the picket lines. Men of his sub-section were saddling their mounts in readiness to depart.

'Right,' he said. 'Malone? Dovey?'

The two men looked over.

'Get the lads to tie their horses to the gun. We're going to be delayed for a bit.'

'What about the gun, Bomb?'

'Lower the poles. It'll take the weight off the horses' shoulders.'

Malone nodded and made his way to the six horse team standing in front of the gun and its limber. 'Give us a hand here, Dovey.'

'I'm going to walk into town. Major Robertshaw wants me to report in with Brigade. Carry on here, Sergeant.'

Richard and Harris saluted Wright, and watched as he walked between the haystacks on the far side of the field before stepping through a gap in the hedge and on up the road.

'I daresay he's really going to get himself a coffee,' said Harris.

'Don't blame him,' said Richard, shaking out the last of his stewed tea. 'Right, I'm going to see a man about a dog, Sergeant.'

Richard collected a small spade from the back of one of the transport wagons and looked around for somewhere private. He smiled. In this fog, he could pretty much drop his trousers anywhere and not be seen. Despite that thought, he walked to the southeast corner of the field, remembering a ditch by the road he'd seen the evening before.

He had remembered right, and he began to unfasten his breeches, looking up and down the road to be sure he wasn't about to be disturbed by a squadron of exercising horses. As he crouched down, he heard the unmistakable sound of a machine-gun. He turned his head to the east from where he felt certain the gunfire originated. He heard shouts coming from the village and from the closer sugar factory as others reacted to the sound of the gun.

He stood and, even as he pulled up his trousers, the first shell struck the Mairie in the village, and then another, closer, exploded, shards of shell-casing whistling overhead.

Richard dropped the spade and clambered out of the shallow ditch. He stared to the east, and there, unbelievably, and no more than half a mile distant, were twelve enemy field guns.

*

Lieutenant Wright was halfway to the Mairie, much looking forward to his coffee, when the first shell struck the village. He didn't realise that's what it was until a moment later when another exploded in the garden. He saw someone thrown to the ground outside the Mairie, and as he ran forward to help, the man stood and climbed onto the back of his horse.

Wright recognised young Thatcher as he tore past down the road on his borrowed grey, and with one last glance towards Brigade HQ, he turned and ran after him.

Harry dragged the reins back, and the grey mare tried to stop in her own body length. She slipped on the damp road surface, but Harry threw himself out of the saddle before she had come to a stop. He looked around for somewhere to tether the horse, but finding nowhere, he just let go of the reins. He stared across at the field and, with rising horror, he realised that the guns could not bear; they were still in lines facing north to south.

'We must get the guns around,' said Wright, running past Harry and clambering through the hedge at the side of the road. The German guns, now clearly visible on the ridge to the east, fired again at the battery, knowing that the small British artillery force was their biggest threat.

The shell arrived well before the sound, and it crashed into the ground a few feet ahead of Wright. His body was torn to fragments by the high-explosive, and there was literally nothing left save a pink smear around the shell hole.

Harry gawped at the scene. Men were desperately trying to bring the guns around, but the horses, terrified of the shelling, were running forwards. They could not move the guns because the poles were still resting on the ground. But they pulled hard, and as they pulled, the poles dug in, knocking the teams from their feet as they tried to escape.

'Cut the traces. Get the horses away. We'll manhandle the guns around.' Rynd and Moore clambered over the fallen team of horses, their knives slashing as they cut the animals free. Some of the horses came to their feet and they ran in all directions; others, their limbs broken, lay where they had fallen.

Richard and Sergeant Harris uncoupled the limber, Moore running over to help. The three dragged the heavy ammunition store out of the way, turning the wheels by pushing and pulling on the spokes.

'Get the guns firing, lads,' said Major Robertshaw, arriving from the sugar factory. The German guns spoke again, more high-explosive shells raining down in the field. Robertshaw was almost up to the gun line when the hot wind of a detonating shell knocked him from his feet. He did not get up.

Other members of the gun crew swarmed over F gun, bringing it around to point to the east.

'Moore, Dovey. Get the ammunition over here,' said Harris.

Quickly, men formed a line and began passing the 13 pound, Mk II Shrapnel rounds from the ammunition limber towards the gun.

'Get some more ammunition from the wagons.'

Sergeant Harris knelt at the trail and looked around, making sure everyone was doing as they should. 'Malone, set the fuze for zero.'

Malone, closest to the limber, turned and nodded, and began to set the timing on the fuze before handing each shell along the line.

Rynd was sitting in the left seat with Moore in the right. The first shell was loaded, and the range set to 800 yards. 'Fire.' The gun crashed out, as did one or two others in the field. Harris watched and could see that the shells were going long. Rynd adjusted the range to 500 yards, and Harris worried for a moment that they would be firing over the heads of the other guns in the field. But there was nothing for it; they hadn't the time to move the gun.

'Fuze to one and a half seconds, Malone.'

The next shell was fired, and this time the shrapnel burst overhead the German gun line. Harris was delighted to see a couple of men go down, but he cursed the British Army decision to provide only shrapnel for their field guns; high-explosive would have been much better.

The Germans were not idle, and a shell struck the muzzle of a British gun, lifting it up and knocking the crew to the ground. Enemy machine-gunners began to pour rounds into the British gun line, the bullets ricocheting off the metal shields of the guns, sending razor-sharp splinters of metal through the air.

Harry didn't know what to do, how he could help. He turned at the sound of horses screaming, and he realised that many of the Queen's Bays' horses were loose, running around the field to the west of the British guns. A shell burst high above the field, the shrapnel balls slashing into the ground below, tearing horseflesh and knocking men down.

One horse in its panic tried to jump over the hedge into the road where Harry stood, but thick blue and pink ropes had caught around its legs and held it fast. Harry recoiled as he realised the ropes were the animal's intestines. He knew he should do something, and he turned to find his own horse, to get his rifle. But there was no sign of the mare.

Another shell screamed overhead, sounding different to the last. It exploded in the line of the Queen's Bays' picketed horses, obliterating three and killing and wounded many more. The men of the Queen's Bays could do nothing more than release their mounts, letting them run away from the danger.

The enemy shellfire was almost incessant now. With each gun able to fire at least once every ten seconds, and usually faster, and with twelve guns in the line, the Germans could fire at least one shell per second onto the British in the village and fields below.

Harry looked back to the field where the British guns were replying to the German fire, and he could see only four were in action. Two were destroyed already, overturned and with their crews dead or wounded around the twisted remains of their gun and limber. Looking beyond the carnage, Harry saw that the Germans intended to bring their cavalry down on the British guns. He saw their horsemen gathering in preparation for a charge from the high ground to the east of the sugar factory.

He turned to look back at the British guns, and then a great gout of earth lurched skyward directly in front of the line. Harry realised it was his brother's gun, and even before

227

the soil had settled, he was running through the hedge and across the field towards the gun.

*

Dovey was dead, his body naked, shorn of its clothes by the high-explosive shell that had killed him. Curiously, thought Richard stepping over the body as he heaved two more shells towards F gun, there was not a mark on him. Killed by concussion, his brain and internal organs had been destroyed inside the shell of flesh.

Richard dropped the shells and turned once more for the limber. He realised it was empty, and he looked around for another source of supply. E gun was the closest, and he could see it was beyond use. He walked towards it.

'Richard!'

He turned at the voice. 'Harry, get yourself out of this field.'

'I want to help.'

'Get away. This is no place for you.'

'I can help.' Harry pulled a shell from the limber by E gun and began to walk over towards F gun. Richard smiled and shook his head, grabbed two shells, and followed his brother back to their own gun. They dropped them and returned immediately to the limber for the rest of the ammunition.

Returning with four more shells, they had just dropped them next to the trail of F gun when a shell struck the shield of another gun. It did not explode, but knocked the gun a few yards back with the force of the impact, slicing into the crew and driving the trail into the body of the commander.

Malone looked at the wreckage of the gun, spotted the piles of unused shells, and ran over. A shrapnel shell burst above him, the heavy balls driving into his body, shattering his skull. He dropped to the ground instantly, and Richard, seeing his friend fall, ran across.

He fell to his knees, turned Malone over, and could see it was hopeless. The right side of his head was missing, and Richard could see into his friend's skull; could see what he knew was his brain. He stood, blood staining his trousers, and stumbled back.

'Get the ammunition,' said Harris from behind him. 'Get the shells. Now!'

Harry put his hand on his brother's shoulder. 'Come on, Richard.'

Richard summoned his mental reserves, and reaching past the twisted corpse, he picked up two shells, turned, and walked back towards their gun. It fired over his head, and he dropped the shells next to Sergeant Harris before turning once more for what was left of D gun.

The Germans on the hillside to the east of the sugar factory brought up their machine-gun company and opened fire at the British artillery. Bullets struck the shield of F gun, and Harris, Rynd and Moore ducked as the bullets clanged and whistled around them.

The number one operating the distant German machine-gun slapped the breech on the left almost imperceptibly, changing the fall of the bullets. Moore was struck by three rounds before the stream of fire moved behind the gun and kicked up the soil around the feet of Harris.

The first round hit Moore in his right shoulder and then struck the breech of the gun where it stopped and fell to the ground. The second sliced through his throat and severed his windpipe. The final bullet hit him low in the left of his ribs. He fell forward against the gun shield, and Harris leaned in to pull him back. The blood frothed at the wound in his neck as Moore struggled to breathe. Blood flowed down into his lungs and he coughed, sending a burst of blood droplets into the air, soaking Harris.

'You,' said Harris, 'pull him out of the way.'

Harry dropped the two shells and moved around the back of the gun. He grasped Moore beneath his shoulders and pulled him clear of the seat. Moore looked up at Harry, tried to speak, but no sound came. Sergeant Harris took up the number two position and he and Rynd worked the gun together.

Harry lay Moore on the ground and held his hand. The cartilage poking out of his neck bubbled with blood as he exhaled, and Harry looked away. Moore gripped Harry's hand tightly and then, a moment later, he relaxed his hold. The blood stopped frothing at the neck wound, and Harry knew he was dead.

'Get more ammunition, boy,' said Harris. 'Now.'

Harry ran over to the nearest upturned gun, but there was nothing left. He looked around the field. He realised that F gun was the only one still in action; the others were either destroyed, or their crews were dead or wounded. He turned towards the sugar factory, remembering that there had been wagons standing there. Perhaps there was ammunition to be found? He began to walk south when a horse came from nowhere, its eyes wild, the stirrups flapping empty against the saddle as it ran in terror. It crashed into Harry and sent him sprawling before continuing past and up towards the road.

Harry groaned and watched the animal running on and then suddenly it was down. It tried to get up, but Harry guessed either its legs were broken or it had some injury to the spine. The front hooves scrabbled uselessly for purchase in the grass, and it whinnied. Harry got to his feet clutching his sides. It hurt to breathe, and he wondered whether he had any broken ribs.

He walked back past the gun line and up to the road. The limber of the last gun in the line had ammunition. He picked up two of the heavy rounds but then he dropped one. He couldn't manage both. He panted with the pain from his ribs, and then he tried again, kneeling to pick up the second round. He struggled back to his feet and walked as quickly as he could manage back to F gun.

Richard had replaced the Harris at the trail, and he took the two rounds from Harry, dropping one to his left. He examined the fuze setting of the other before handing it to Harris for loading. No sooner had the breech block been slammed shut than the gun was fired, and Richard reached for the next round.

The Germans had realised that all other British guns were out of action. With only one remaining target, the Germans flailed the field around F gun with shrapnel. A ball struck Harris in the head; a glancing blow, but enough to open his forehead and send blood streaming into his eyes. 'I can't see to load,' he said. 'Thatcher, you get up here and I'll help your brother find ammunition.'

Harris stepped back and began to follow Harry across towards the furthest British gun in the line. A high-explosive shell struck the ground halfway between them. The blast sliced off Harris's legs midway between knee and thigh and took away his right arm. Harry was thrown down by the force of the blast. He lay dazed for some moments, and gradually his hearing cleared and his senses returned. He remembered where he was, what was happening.

He rolled over and stared across the ruined field. The haystacks had been reduced to low piles, the gun line was in chaos, and everywhere were dead and dying men and horses. He looked at F gun, alone in the line, firing up at the German gunners and cavalry, and somehow keeping them at bay.

Harry stood and walked back towards the gun. He tripped over something in the grass, and looking down, he saw it was a human leg, complete with boot and sock. He walked on and found the rest of Sergeant Harris. Kneeling over the man, Harry realised he still lived, although how was anyone's guess.

'Take me to the gun, lad. Take me to the gun.'

Harry nodded, and getting behind the sergeant, he dragged his body, setting him down against the wheel of the gun's limber which could offer him some protection from the fierce enemy fire.

'Cover my legs, lad. Don't want to upset the boys,' said Harris, and Harry looked about. He saw a discarded blanket a few yards away and went for it. He placed the blanket over the tattered stumps of the sergeant's legs. 'Now, go and help your brother. I'll be fine here.'

Harry nodded and returned to the gun.

'Are there any more shells, Harry?'

Harry looked back up the field to the gun by the road. He knew there were a few more up there. He nodded and then made for the distant gun. In truth, it was no more than thirty or forty yards, but that's a long way when the ground is being torn to pieces by enemy gunfire.

Arriving at the limber, he saw there were half a dozen shells remaining. He realised that meant three trips across the field, and no one's luck could last that long. He looked about. A dead horse lay nearby, and Harry edged over towards it, keeping low to the ground. Crouching behind the carcass, he unfastened the bedding roll and took off the groundsheet. He was sliding back across the ground towards the limber when he heard a voice.

'Water.'

Harry looked about but could see no one.

'Water. Please.'

He glanced beneath the limber and there he saw a wounded gunner. 'I have no water,' said Harry.

'Water.'

Harry looked back across at the gun. He could see a corpse lying near the trail. He crawled over. The man did not have a water bottle, and Harry cursed. He searched around the gun for a bottle, but couldn't find one. He crawled back over to the limber. 'I can't find any.'

There was no response.

Harry knelt up and working as quick as he could, he pulled out the six shells and placed them onto the groundsheet. Then he began to edge backwards on the ground, dragging the ammunition behind him. He dug his heels into the soil and heaved, crying out as his ribs grated. Slowly, he covered the distance, but it took him fully five minutes to get back to his brother and F gun.

'Thank the Lord,' said Richard. 'We're down to the last few shells.'

Rynd turned to take up the next shell and a sliver of shell casing struck his neck, slicing through muscle and bone before striking Richard's left elbow. Rynd's head fell to the ground, rolling so that his eyes stared upwards. Harry looked down at the surprised look on Rynd's face. Rynd blinked his eyes once, and Harry retched, the bile rising in his throat.

Rynd's body lolled forwards and then toppled back, his bottom still on the layer's seat. His shoulders struck the ground and his heart pumped for a few more beats, blood gushing onto the grass at Harry's feet. Harry tore his eyes away from the severed head and looked to his brother. 'Are you hurt, Richard?'

Richard clutched his elbow. 'I'll live,' he said with more bravado than he felt. He looked over at Rynd's body. 'Get behind the shield, Harry. We'll fire off our last few rounds and then we can do no more.' Richard glanced up at the hill to their southeast. The German cavalry were coming down the hillside to finish what the artillery had started. If they had more men, they could get the gun around onto the enemy horsemen, but there was no way the two of them could manage it.

Harry nodded. He picked up a shell and they loaded the gun. No sooner was it ready than they fired, sending another shrapnel shell on the same trajectory as all the others. It went longer because the barrel was hot, now, but it was still creating devastation up in the German gun line.

'This is the last, Richard,' said Harry a few minutes later. Richard nodded, and then he shut the breech block. The gun fired and then was silent. There was nothing for them to do, now, except keep their heads down. And there was nothing stopping the German advance, so their cavalry cantered down the slope towards the sugar factory and the field to its north.

Twenty

'We can't sit and do nothing, Richard. I'm going to find more ammunition. I haven't tried the gun furthest from the road. I don't think it even came into action. There might be shells there.'

'It's too dangerous, Harry. Stay here. We've done our bit.'

'I won't be long.' He stood and dashed around the end of the gun shield. He looked ahead, and the furthest gun seemed a long way away. Having said he'd go, he couldn't seem to make his legs move.

'Stay here, Harry.'

But Harry was off and running. He thought perhaps he should move side to side to make himself a difficult target, but he decided to trust to fate and take the shortest and fastest route. He jumped a fallen horse and passed the first gun. Two more to go.

Out of the corner of his eyes he could see men watching him as he passed; men sensibly huddled beneath their broken guns and shattered ammunition limbers. With no guns, there was little point in exposing themselves to enemy gunfire. He passed the second gun, and it seemed the Germans would let him get all the way there safely.

His arms and legs pumped as he ran, his lungs bursting with the effort. Never had he run so fast. The last gun lay just ahead, overturned by a high-explosive shell. The crew lay about it, all dead so far as Harry could tell. The limber, upside down, lay to the left of the gun. Harry knelt behind it and saw that it contained a good few shells. He looked back to F gun. He doubted he would make it if he crawled, dragging the ammunition as he had earlier. He would just take two and run for it.

He pulled out a shell and laid it on the grass. He was just removing a second round when a voice came from behind. 'Is your gun still firing, then?'

Harry turned and looked at the man who had spoken. An officer. 'Yes, Sir.'

The lieutenant looked over to a sergeant huddling behind a dead horse. 'Sergeant? Let's take two shells each and cut along to this lad's gun.'

The sergeant stood and ran forwards, crouching next to Harry. 'Give me four,' he said. Harry loaded the man's broad arms with the ammunition. Over fifty pounds weight, and awkward to carry, too. The sergeant turned to leave.

'Hang on,' said the lieutenant, taking two shells from the limber. 'We should all go together.'

The sergeant nodded. Harry loaded the lieutenant's arms with two shells and then he took two for himself, one tucked under each arm.

'Right,' said the lieutenant. 'Let's go.' He stood, and capricious fate intervened: the Germans chose that moment to open fire. A shrapnel shell detonated overhead. The sergeant grunted, but kept to his feet. He waited no more, turning and staggering off up the field towards F gun. The lieutenant had a funny look on his face, and the shells he had been carrying dropped to the ground. He slipped to his knees and toppled forwards. Harry couldn't wait. He looked at the two discarded shells, decided he couldn't manage more, and turned to run after the sergeant.

He passed the big man within a few moments and ran on, covering the distance to Richard and the waiting gun surprisingly quickly. The Germans fired again and again, seeing men moving around the guns and determined to remove the threat the artillery still posed.

Men of the enemy cavalry stared at the British guns, wanting to take them; there was great honour to be had in capturing enemy guns. There was only one remaining, they could see, but one was still worth the risk. They urged their horses down the hill and couched their lances beneath their elbows, ready to drive the enemy artillerymen away from the prizes they coveted.

Harry dropped the two shells and turned to go back for the others that the sergeant was bringing up more slowly. He was halfway back when the sergeant disappeared in a hail of shrapnel. His body was cut to ribbons. Harry hesitated, looking towards the dead sergeant and his precious ammunition, and then another shell burst above him, and he felt the wind of shrapnel all around him. He wasn't hit, but he decided enough was enough. He turned to run back to the meagre shelter of the gun.

Richard managed to get a round off at the German gunners, and then another shrapnel shell burst above them. Harry threw himself to the ground behind the gun, seeking the cover of the shield and the heavy breech block. Rynd's headless body, still hanging from the number one's seat, was flayed by shrapnel.

'That was close,' he said, looking over to Richard. But Richard wasn't in his seat any longer. The last shell burst had hit him hard, and he lay on the ground by the trail of the gun. Harry shuffled over on his knees towards his brother. 'Richard?'

Richard opened an eye. 'Harry?' Thick, dark blood dribbled from the corner of his mouth as he spoke, running slowly down his cheek.

'I'm here, Richard.' He looked at his brother's mutilated body and then reached out and took hold of the bloody stump of his left arm. He looked up to the east, and he saw the German cuirassiers coming across the field unopposed, driving their lances into men hiding behind the guns and heading towards Harry and the last remaining British gun. 'I'm here,' he said again.

*

Harry knew they would be captured. He laughed a hollow, bitter laugh. After all his efforts to keep one step ahead of the Germans, it would all end here. He might as well have given himself up back at the sugar factory a week ago.

A German horseman spotted Harry and swerved around an overturned transport wagon and then jumped a dead horse without taking his eyes off his target. Harry watched the lance tip as the man straightened his arm, ready to spear the last defender of the last British gun.

Harry looked around for a weapon, but he could see nothing. And then he remembered Carmichael's pistol. He glanced down and began to unfasten his haversack, his fingers fumbling with the brass fastenings in his haste, before reaching in for the Webley.

The cuirassier was almost on them, and he was smiling. Harry's arm came up, and the horseman saw the handgun at the last moment. The pistol kicked hard in Harry's hand, and the heavy bullet struck the horseman in his chest. His lance tip clipped the gun's wheel, a glancing blow, and then the dead German was past, his horse carrying his corpse on across the field.

But there were more coming, and Harry fired again and again without apparent effect until the hammer fell on an empty chamber with a click. He tossed the Webley aside, and watched another cuirassier coming on.

The horseman could see Harry was the last defender of the last gun of the battery, and he would capture it from him. He gripped the wooden shaft of his lance, leaned from the saddle, and made ready to drive the tip through the artilleryman's body.

Harry looked up at the German's face, and knew there was nothing he could do. And then the German and his horse were gone; snatched away by a hail of lead balls. The crash of a British thirteen pounder reached Harry's ears, and he knelt up, trying to locate the sound. The guns, wherever they were, fired again and again, clearing the field of the enemy horsemen. The German cavalry stalled in the face of the bombardment. There was no point dying to take the last gun. They galloped out of danger and headed back up to the eastern ridge.

Harry came to his feet and looked west, and there he saw another British horse artillery battery. Six guns firing between them up to ninety rounds a minute, and now it was the Germans' turn to feel the horror of constant enemy artillery fire. One by one, the German guns stopped firing as the men servicing them died or ran after the retreating cavalry.

There was an attempt to retrieve the guns, the German riders bravely coming forward to try to limber them up and ride them to safety, but the British fire was murderous on the ridge, and soon there were not enough horses left to pull the guns. Those that could, rode away.

All this, Harry could not see. He crouched low over his brother's body and held his arm. He could see that he still lived because there was the gentle beat of his heart showing in the veins of his neck. But Richard didn't speak. He never opened his eyes again. But afterwards, Harry liked to think that he knew that he had been there with him. At the end.

*

'Jesus Christ,' said Thomson. He stood at the edge of the field and looked at the devastation wrought by the German guns. He had delivered his message, and the infantry had come barrelling down the road as fast as they could, and the cavalry had arrived with another battery of guns. And although they had seen off an entire enemy cavalry division, they had been too late to save L Battery.

'Have you seen young Thatcher?' said Major Allen.

'No. I left him at the Mairie hours ago.'

'I expect he's down there.'

Thomson looked at the field again. Only one gun remained in service, and it had no crew left. The field was littered with dead and dying horses, their bodies cruelly maimed. Unable to get free from their harnesses, they had been cut to shreds by the shellfire.

Here and there a shot rang out as another animal was put out of its misery. But for the wounded men, no less horribly hurt, there was no such easy exit. An aid post was established in the sugar factory, and men were carried off the field to the doctors. Those beyond help were given pain relief and left to slip away.

'With his brother,' added the major.

Thomson turned and stared at Allen. Then he was running across the narrow road and through the hedge. He sprinted along the gun line, stopping at each khaki bundle to see if it contained the body of his friend.

'Harry,' he said, finally spotting the youngster sitting with his back against the wheel of F gun, his hand holding the bloodied sleeve of a dead artilleryman.

Harry didn't respond. He stared into the middle distance without seeing. Thomson knelt in front of him and looked into his eyes. Recognition crossed his features, and Harry looked at Thomson. 'He's dead. The Germans killed my brother.'

'Come on; let's get you out of here, Harry.'

'I can't leave him. I won't.'

'Then we'll take him with us.'

They walked across the field towards the sugar factory, Thomson cradling Richard's broken body in his arms while Harry walked next to him.

Epilogue

The major's boots crunched in the snow, now some inches deep on the hidden duck-boards. He pulled his greatcoat collar tight around his neck and was glad of the scarf his wife had sent out with the hamper earlier in the week.

'Trooper Thomson.' Allen's breath misted in the air around his face as he spoke.

'Sir,' said Thomson, saluting. 'You'll find the dug-out yonder, Sir,' he added, pointing to his left.

Allen returned the salute. 'It's fearful cold.'

'You should try one of these, Sir. They're all the rage.' Thomson turned around slowly so that Major Allen could admire his goatskin jerkin.

'It makes you smell like a farmyard, though, Thomson.'

Thomson sniffed the cold air. 'I suppose it does, Sir.' He grinned.

'Merry Christmas, Thomson.'

'And you, Sir.'

Allen walked down the trench passing men huddled against the walls, trying to keep out of the wind. Each firebay was manned by several troopers, one or more of whom was taking their turn at watch up on the firestep, staring out over the darkness of no man's land.

He reached the dug-out that served as the squadron headquarters when they were in the line. Someone had attached a sprig of holly to the rough timber frame of the doorway. Music was coming from inside. Allen smiled, and then ducked through the doorway.

'Sir.' Captain Embury came to his feet.

'Mozart, Captain?' said Allen, coming down a few short steps. 'A little Teutonic, perhaps?'

'He was an Austrian, Sir.'

'Last time I checked, they were on the other side.' Allen looked around the small room, dug into soil at the back of the trench. A Fortnum and Mason's hamper, much like the one his wife had sent out, stood on a table in the corner, the gramophone on a chair next to it.

'A glass of brandy, Sir?'

'No, thank you, Captain,' said Allen. 'I have my own medicinal supplies,' he added, patting his greatcoat pocket. 'And nothing so continental. Good Irish whiskey.'

'You'll need a dram on a night like tonight.'

'Corporal Pike won't be re-joining the Regiment, Captain.'

'Oh?'

'His wounds mean that he won't see active service again, but I understand he has accepted a training post.'

'Good news,' said Embury, relieved that the unpopular NCO would not be returning.

'Have you seen your acting corporal?'

'He's in the next firebay along, Sir.'

'I think you can confirm his promotion.'

'Yes, Sir.'

Allen took one final look around, took in the books on the shelves and the picture of Embury's wife in a silver frame over by the cot. He nodded. 'Carry on, Captain.'

Allen took the next turn to the left, into a traverse, and then right again into another firebay. Trenches were constructed with these turns to minimise the casualties caused when a shell landed in a trench – and to make capturing the trench more difficult for an attacker.

Up ahead, sitting in a recess cut from the clay of the parados, or rear wall of the trench, a man was sitting, his knees drawn up. Allen could see he had been there a while; snow had settled across his legs to some depth. Despite the bitter cold, Allen could see that he was writing. He walked closer. 'A letter home, Corporal?'

The corporal folded the scrap of paper in half and slipped it into his greatcoat pocket before turning to look at Allen. 'Yes, Sir,' he said, although it wasn't.

'I've just come from Regimental HQ. You've got some leave due, Thatcher.'

'Leave?'

'Yes. A week in London. Hearth and home and all that.'

Harry frowned. Home. He didn't give it much thought, these days.

'When, Sir?'

'Day after Boxing Day. Three days' time, in case you've forgotten it's Christmas Eve.'

Harry nodded. 'I don't have to go home, though, do I, Sir?'

Allen looked at the young man. He had changed so much in the last four months. 'No, not if you don't want. We can write out a travel warrant for wherever you want to go.'

'I've never seen Paris, Sir. I thought perhaps…'

'Good idea. New Year's eve in Paris. All those young French girls and you in your new corporal's chevrons. They'll find you irresistible, Corporal. Do you know, perhaps I shall join you?'

Harry smiled a smile that went nowhere near his eyes.

'Well, drop by Regimental HQ, Corporal, and we'll see about that warrant. You're moving out of the line tomorrow night.'

The two looked at one another. 'Well, I'd better get back. Stilton cheese won't eat itself, and my wife sent a good supply.'

'Merry Christmas, Sir.'

Allen headed back the way he had come, and Harry watched him until a swirl of snow hid him from view. Harry looked around. Over by Christmas, he thought, and not for the first time that day. Still, he supposed, they had a few hours left. He wondered whether he should check on his men, but it was a quiet night.

He climbed back into his funk hole, keen to get out of the worst of the weather, and took out the letter to Geneviève. He had written to her often, sometimes as much as three or four times a week. He had never got a reply, but he told himself it was because his letters had got lost. He knew that had she received them, she would have written back to him.

He began writing, and then he stopped and listened. He could hear voices; singing voices. He recognised the tune: Silent Night, but the words were being sung in German. He pushed the letter back into his pocket and stood up, grabbing his rifle. He climbed up onto the firestep next to trooper Williams.

'Alright, Corporal?'

'Anything happening out there?'

The two stared across no man's land. Nothing seemed to be moving.

'No, Corporal.'

The German voices carried across on the wind once more. 'Did you hear that?'

'Yes, Corporal. Jerry's been at it all night.'

'Singing?'

'Yes.'

'What's that?' Harry stared across the short stretch of frozen mud that separated the two armies. He had seen a flickering light, and suspecting an attack, he checked his weapon was loaded.

'I think it's a candle, Corporal.'

Whatever it was, the wind soon snuffed it out, but a moment later, more flickering lights appeared on the enemy parapet. 'What's he doing?' said Harry.

'Hey, Tommy!'

Harry brought his rifle to his shoulder and aimed down the sights. 'Go and get Captain Embury, Williams.'

Williams jumped down from the firestep and ran along the firebay towards the dug-out.

Harry stared across at the candles. There was no doubt, that's what they were.

'Tommy, you want a cigar?'

Harry couldn't believe it. Some kind of trick? But why would they announce themselves?

'We have Stollen and brandy.'

A figure moved on the far parapet, and Harry squeezed the trigger. The round whistled into the darkness. 'Don't shoot! We are coming up.'

Harry felt he was losing control of the situation. 'Get back,' he said, screaming. He fired again.

'Tommy, we are friends tonight. It is Christmas, yes? We will come up.'

'No, you bloody well won't. Keep you heads down, or I'll blow them off,' said Harry, switching to German without thinking about it. He fired wildly into the night again. The Germans did nothing further for a while, and then there was singing again.

'What's going on, Corporal?'

Harry turned to see both Captain Embury and Thomson on the duck-boards below.

'Jerry wants to share his Christmas cake with us, Sir.'

'He what?'

'Stollen and brandy, Sir.'

Embury thought about it. 'And that was you firing, Corporal?'

'Yes, Sir.'

'Well, let's see what happens.' He climbed up onto the step and stood beside Harry. 'What are those?'

'Candles, Sir.'

Embury looked at him.

The carol came to an end, and there was laughter from the far trench. Then the same voice from earlier carried across to them. 'Don't shoot, Tommy. I come out by myself.'

A moment later, a figure appeared on the enemy parapet. Harry brought his rifle to his shoulder and lowered his head to take aim.

'Wait,' said Embury.

Harry relaxed his finger on the trigger and lifted his head. He looked across the short gap. The German was coming across no man's land. His hands were up, and so far as Harry could see, he carried no weapons. He walked until he was about halfway, and then stopped.

'You come out. The one who speaks German.'

'You been talking to them, Corporal?' said Embury, grinning.

'I told them to keep their heads down, Sir.'

'I think you should go.'

'What?'

'What harm could there be in it?'

'It might be some kind of attack, Sir.'

'It might, but it seems a strange way to go about it. Thomson will cover you.'

Thomson climbed up onto the firestep and cocked his rifle. 'I've got you, Corporal.'

Harry looked at Embury, then Thomson and finally at the gormless Williams who grinned up at him from the trench floor.

'Bring me back some cake, Corporal,' said Williams.

'I can't believe I'm doing this.' Harry leant his rifle against the trench wall and pulled himself up onto the sandbags on top of the parapet. He stood motionless for a moment, waiting for the fusillade of German gunfire that would be his end. Nothing happened. The German standing ahead waved him over. 'Come.'

Harry swallowed, and then stepped forwards, his boots cracking the rime that had formed over the snow. The German lowered his hands to his sides as Harry approached, but nothing happened, and Harry reached him without incident.

The man nodded and smiled. 'Merry Christmas, Tommy.'

'My name is not Tommy, it's Harry.'

'I am Tobias.' He held out his hand. Harry ignored it, but the German seemed to take no offence and shrugged, dropping his hand to his side again.

The two stood and stared, their uniform colours marking them as enemies.

'Alright, Corporal Thatcher?'

Harry turned to speak over his shoulder. 'Yes, Sir.'

'I'm coming out.'

Harry and the German, Tobias, watched as Embury pulled himself over the parapet; no easy task without a ladder. And then Harry noticed other figures along the German line clambering out of their trench.

'Sir? They're all coming.'

Embury paused, but after a moment, he decided it would be alright and walked forwards. He arrived next to Harry, his breathing hard and fast with the fear of the moment. It was no easy thing to stand thus exposed in no man's land.

Tobias introduced himself.

'Cecil Embury.' The two shook hands.

Thomson appeared from the darkness, Williams just behind, and within moments, there were dozens of men standing in the gap between the trenches.

Tobias offered Embury a cigar, as promised, and the delighted captain leaned in towards another German soldier for a light, puffing contentedly.

Williams came across to Harry, his mouth full, his lips coated with icing sugar. 'Fantastic fruit cake, Corporal,' he said, spitting pieces of almond slice over Harry's greatcoat as he spoke.

Men were exchanging hats, swapping photographs and struggling to understand each other. Flasks of whiskey and of schnapps made the rounds.

It was all getting a little too friendly for Harry, and he stepped backwards, his eyes fixed on the Germans in the crowd that had formed in no man's land.

'Where are you going, Harry?' said Tobias, spotting the British corporal heading back to his own trench.

Harry stopped at the voice. Then he turned back and walked away. Thomson caught him up and put a hand on his arm. 'Harry?'

'Leave me alone, Trooper.'

'They're just being friendly.'

'Are they? You remember the farmer's wife?'

Thomson hesitated a moment. 'That was one man. They've no more desire to be here than we have. And it is Christmas.'

'You enjoy your party, Thomson. But when tomorrow comes, we'll be trying to kill the beggars, and they will try to kill us.'

'Perhaps not? Maybe this means something?'

Harry turned to face his friend. 'Do you really think that GHQ, or the politicians that got us into this, are going to let us fraternise with the Germans? Let us shake their hands and make friends? Call the whole thing off?' He laughed and began to climb back down into the British trench.

'They're only men, Harry. Same as us.'

Harry looked back up at Thomson. 'Are they?' he said, and then he was gone.

Author's note

Virtually everything described in this book happened in the opening weeks of the war, although I have changed the names of those involved (with the exception General Allenby and Brigadier Briggs) to give me a bit of latitude; call it artistic licence, if you like. For the most part, the story follows the exploits of the men of the 4th Royal Irish Dragoon Guards, part of the 2nd Cavalry Brigade.

In late August, the small but well-trained British Expeditionary Force advanced, met with the numerically superior Germans, and were forced to disengage. They then endured a long retreat of over a hundred miles, almost to Paris, with the Germans snapping at their heels the whole way.

Some British units were destroyed and many others suffered horrendous losses. But through courage, gritty determination, some miscalculation by the Germans and no small amount of luck, they held the enemy back.

*

I believe that the *Action at Néry*, as the battle is often called, was pivotal to the outcome of the Great War, despite the relatively small numbers of troops and casualties involved. The damage inflicted by the British 1st Cavalry

Brigade on the German 4th Cavalry Division meant that the latter could no longer participate in the advance on Paris.

The temporary loss of the German division weakened the German II Cavalry Corps and slowed its advance. Consequently, the French Fifth Army were able to avoid destruction and escape across the Marne. In addition, the defenders of Paris had time and resources to build-up their defences.

As Lyn Macdonald says in her book, 1914: The days of hope:

"Néry was destined to be the 'horseshoe nail' which in the course of a very few days would puncture the balloon of (German) plans and aspirations and decide the final outcome of the Battle of the Marne."

It was at the Marne that the Allies halted the German advance and stopped the headlong allied retreat. Had they failed to do this, Germany would almost certainly have won the war in those opening weeks. As it was, the war against Germany was not won; rather, it was not lost.

*

At Saint-Quentin, the real life Lieutenant-Colonel Mainwaring (1st Battalion, Royal Warwickshire Regiment) and Lieutenant-Colonel Elkington (2nd Battalion, Royal Dublin Fusiliers) probably felt they had little choice but to surrender their exhausted and depleted battalions. Both were cashiered from the army a few weeks after the retreat from Mons. Elkington later returned to France to fight with great courage as an ordinary solider with the French Foreign Legion, regaining his honour.

The battle that takes place at the end of the story, at Néry, is based on fact, although, of course, neither Thomson nor

Harry had any business being there. L Battery of the Royal Horse Artillery (1st Cavalry Brigade) did much to help to overcome a numerically superior enemy. The battery lost all its officers and a quarter of its men during the three hour action, and three Victoria Crosses (VCs) were won by Captain Bradbury (who died during the battle), Sergeant-Major Dorrell and Sergeant Nelson (both survived the battle, but Sergeant Nelson was killed later in the war). You can see their VCs, together with a surviving gun from L Battery, at the Imperial War Museum in London.

The first winners of a VC during the Great War were Lieutenant Maurice Dease and Private Sidney Godley, both of 4th Battalion, Royal Fusiliers. I mentioned their brave defence of Nimy Bridge, Mons, in the story. Dease was killed and Godley taken prisoner, but the rest of their Battalion got away to fight another day.

*

I took the liberty of making a few changes to help my story along for which I apologise. Firstly, the inn which served such wonderful and seemingly never ending omelettes was not located south of Saint-Quentin as I portrayed it, but south of Le Cateau.

Secondly, although the cavalry were to spend an increasing amount of their time in the trenches as infantry soldiers, I am uncertain whether the 4th Dragoon Guards were in the line during Christmas, 1914. But as I wanted Harry to meet a German, that's where I put them.

Finally, the attack by the German cuirassiers on L Battery did not reach as far as the field itself, being held back by rifle and well-sited machine-gun fire from dismounted British troops in the village.

Acknowledgements

I have read many books about the Great War, but these were my constant companions during this project: Riding the Retreat, Richard Holmes; 1914: The days of hope, Lyn MacDonald; The Affair at Nery, Patrick Takle; Horsemen in No Man's Land, David Kenyan; Record of the 4th Royal Irish Dragoon Guards in the Great War 1914-1918, Rev. Harold Gibb; Christmas Truce, Malcolm Brown and Shirley Seaton.

I'd also like to thank Rosie Whitaker for her help and advice on shotguns, most of which went over my head.

30992525R00154

Made in the USA
Charleston, SC
02 July 2014